Hanover Square Spare

Rakes of Rotten Row

Hanover Square Spare

Copyright 2023 by In For A Penny Publishing, LLC and Annabelle Anders

All rights reserved.

This is a work of fiction. Names, places, characters, and events are fictitious in every regard. Any similarities to actual events and persons, living or dead, are purely coincidental. Any trademarks, service marks, product names, or named features are assumed to be the property of their respective owners, and are used only for reference. There is no implied endorsement if any of these terms are used. Except for review purposes, the reproduction of this book in whole or part, electronically or mechanically, constitutes a copyright violation.

Cover by Barbara Cantor, Forever After Romance Designs.

❦ Created with Vellum

MARRIAGE OF CONVENIENCE * LITTLE SISTER * SPARE TURNED HEIR

The Earl of Standish couldn't have a worse name. He's not in good standing anywhere, but with luck and the right bride, that should all change...

As the Duke of Crossing's overlooked daughter, Lady Marigold Hathaway's prospects are limited, at best. So when Lord Standish comes to her with a shocking proposition, she can't help but consider it.

When everyone has always wanted her older sister, why would this handsome earl suddenly want her? And does it matter, seeing as she was halfway to falling in with him anyway?

Hanover Square Spare was initially titled, Earl of Standish, and was published on Jan.3, 2023, in *Wicked Earls Forever*. This edition includes exclusive **bonus content** and is book 1 of Annabelle Anders' newest series, *Rakes of Rotten Row*.

BY ANNABELLE ANDERS

TWO HEADLINES

Reed Rutherford, the Earl of Standish now, stepped into the foyer of the club he'd only heard of before: *The Domus Emporium*—a discreet gentlemen's club set just outside of Mayfair.

Inhaling, Reed detected the scent that was uniquely male and uniquely noble—a subtle blend of cigar smoke, scotch, and expensive colognes he'd always associated with his uncle.

Until recently, he'd only heard of the club from his less-than-upstanding male relatives—now, all dead. A disturbing wave of emptiness washed over him, but he ignored it and took in his surroundings. The understated luxury consisted of gleaming mahogany tables and furnishings upholstered with either leather or forest-green velvet. Two or three dozen candles burned overhead, secured in an understated chandelier dangling from the high ceiling.

A few ladies mingled amongst them, dressed in finery and jewels that would put any duchess to shame. It was the intelligence in their eyes, however, that truly set them apart from ladies of the *ton*.

That and the fact that they made their living providing all manner of sexual favors.

As Reed picked his way between the felt-covered tables, patrons gradually became aware of his presence, and the low murmurs fell silent. Sharp eyes followed him, and an oppressive hush settled upon the room.

But he would not be cowed, and he narrowed his gaze when an annoying voice cut through the tension.

"What have we here, fellows, but the new Earl of Standish?" The Marquess of Pittsguard, or "Pitt" as he was known, lifted a snifter in Reed's direction. The seams on the balding lord's jacket strained against the padding in his shoulders, and if the shirt points on his collar were any higher, they'd likely put the man's eyes out.

Reed kept his expression bland. He was not fool enough to see the toast for anything other than the mockery intended.

"How lucky for you, *Standish*," a second voice leered. "I can only dream that the seven blokes standing between myself and my great uncle's title would vanish as conveniently as yours have." Mr. Marshall, one of the younger gentlemen present, raised his glass as well. His hooded eyes and wobbling stance revealed that although it was barely noon, he was already deep into his cups.

Glancing around, Reed realized most of them were in a similar condition.

Likely, they'd been at it all night.

Reed, of course, was stone-cold sober. Despite his new waistcoat, shining Hessians, and perfectly tied cravat, he wasn't one of them.

"Indeed," he addressed Marshall, the word dripping in sarcasm, "but not everyone can be so lucky." Fists clenched at his sides, he was prepared to make the next heckler pay.

Luck—a ridiculous word to describe the tragedy his family had experienced over the past month.

Reed hated being the subject of attention. He far preferred holing up in Rutherford Place, the century-old Standish Mayfair townhouse discreetly set back from the street across from Hanover Square. He'd prefer to be anywhere else, actually, sorting out estate accounts, or even addressing the abundance of vowels he'd inherited along with the title.

And that was precisely what he'd be doing if not for the urgent message he'd received from his long-time trusted friend, Jasper Perry, the Baron of Westcott. Considered to be something of a philanderer, some referred to West as the Piccadilly Player. *Ludicrous.* Reed pinched his mouth flat. All it had taken were a few dubious accusations from a scorned debutante's mama and the nickname had stuck.

Which was only one of the reasons Reed had avoided Mayfair as long as he had.

Reed searched the room, eager to find the fellow and learn what could possibly merit such urgency.

Having *benefitted* from the recent demise of his uncle, cousin, older brother, and father, he'd suspected there would be rumors. Any man in his situation would find himself under intense speculation and scrutiny.

Damn, damn, and double damn.

Because, despite four healthy male relatives having stood between himself and the title, Reed was Standish now—as in *Lord Standish.*

As in, the *bloody Earl of Standish*. Something he'd never wished for or wanted.

All four men had perished in the fire that had consumed the hunting cabin at Searidge Manor, his uncle's estate.

Hell, now it was *his* estate.

And although the cause of death listed on their certificates was accurate, it was but a small part of the story.

Only a handful of people comprehended the vices practiced by the recently deceased—and how those depravities had come into play. They'd all been incoherent—out of their heads from the combination of opium and alcohol they favored. Even less had heard his uncle's recent ramblings of ending it all—of escaping this world permanently. Had it been an accident? If just one of them had been even partly conscious, the fire could have been extinguished.

At the very least, they could have escaped and lived to tempt fate some other time in the future.

Reed refused to mourn them. Hell, he hadn't time to mourn them—what with fielding the massive debts they'd left behind.

Debts beyond comprehension. Disgruntled tenants. Unpaid vendors. Gambling vowels.

Not to mention the care of his mother and three sisters. His uncle's wife had departed the estate the day following the funeral, announcing she'd rather live with her sister than remain at Seabridge Manor another day. For which Reed had been grateful.

One less burden for him to bear.

Because his mother and sisters had been left distraught in the wake of the tragedy. His mother had cared about her husband and loved Randal, her oldest son. Reed's sisters had looked to the two men for security, until recently.

But for the most part, they had been left reeling by the loss of their father and eldest brother.

Reed clenched and then unclenched his fists. He could not dwell on them now. He had far more pressing issues to sort out.

Blasted issues none of them had considered before acting so recklessly.

The most urgent of which was this unsavory scandal. By revealing as few details of the fire as possible, by declining any further investigation that might expose his uncle's dark comments, Reed himself had fallen under suspicion.

And ridicule.

And a few legal challenges.

But it was best this way. He'd bury the unsavory circumstances of their deaths right along with them. No one need ever suspect the worst.

Caroline, Melanie, and Josephine's innocent faces came to mind. The rumors about Reed's part in all of it would die down and then he could go about salvaging his sisters' futures. If anything else got out, the poor girls would forever live as pariahs.

"Rutherford." A friendly face appeared, loosening the vise that had begun to tighten around Reed's chest. Westcott and Reed had been in the same level at Eton and, together, had fought off more than one bully. "Right on time." West jerked his head toward a darkened corner near the back of the room. Upon closer inspection, Reed could see a set of heavy velvet drapes hanging there, likely concealing a back entrance.

Reed exhaled.

Not at all reluctant to absent himself from dubious happenings around the gaming tables, Reed shook the hand West offered and followed him away from the main area.

"Good to see you," he said. Relieved as he was, Reed was still keenly aware that West had refused to share with him the purpose of this meeting. The continued secrecy only further fueled his curiosity.

"Likewise, my friend." West glanced over his shoulder with a warm smile. The baron hadn't changed much in the past few years. He was still slim and broad-shouldered, one of the rare noblemen never to have worn padding. He had hair that alternately appeared light brown and dark blond, and hazel eyes, making the man something of a chameleon.

Stepping through the heavy curtains, Reed followed West up a spiraling staircase to a carpeted foyer. On one side, a wall, on the other, a gleaming railing that overlooked the main floor of the club. West marched to the end of the foyer, and knocked on the heavy wooden door. Without waiting for an answer, he pushed it open and gestured for Reed to precede him inside.

Knowing the Duke of Malum owned the club, Reed immediately guessed this to be the infamous duke's personal office. Hints of cigar smoke blended with lemon oil, mahogany, leather, and an unrecognizable spice. On one side of the office, a massive desk. On the other, a comfortably arranged seating area where hot coals burned in the adjacent hearth.

As Reed perused the faces of the occupants, the hairs on the back of his neck stood up.

Despite having kept mostly absent from society, he had, however, kept abreast of happenings via the newspapers. He'd seen the caricatures and recognized all but one of the gentlemen lounging there—a handful of the most powerful men in all of England.

And not one of them appeared welcoming. What the hell was West up to?

His old friend gestured toward two of them. "Standish, you know Helton and Winterhope." Maxwell Black, the Earl of Helton, lived year-round in London and had recently entered the London Gazette. The man's black hair was unkempt and he looked not to have shaved in two or three days. Nonetheless, intelligent green eyes met Reed's from behind a pair of spectacles.

With the earl having taken permanent residence in London, Reed wondered at the condition of the man's country estate. Had he simply abandoned it?

"Helton," Reed leaned forward, noting ink stains on the man's hand as he shook it.

He then turned to Benjamin St. Lancaster, the Marquess of Winterhope and owner of England's finest stables, Hope Downs. With neatly trimmed brown hair and sideburns, the man's flamboyant suit fit him like a glove, and his cravat was tied perfectly. Winterhope's appearance contrasted sharply with that of the earl's.

"You're looking nobbish," Winterhope observed. The comment came as no surprise to Reed, but even having been dressed in the latest finery—by his dead cousin's valet—he'd yet to feel comfortable in his new position.

And damned if he ever would.

Before Reed could respond, West gestured toward the seedier-looking of the other two gentlemen. Although the hulking fellow appeared relaxed, with one booted foot resting on his knee, the man's eyes burned with a cunning intensity. "Mr. Beckworth," West introduced the man without further explanation.

And none was needed. Reed had heard of Leopold Beckworth. The man, known to be ruthless and calculating, likely controlled half the commerce that took place on the docks. When they shook hands, Reed found Beckworth's grip to be firm, his hands, scarred and rugged.

"And, of course, Malum."

Whereas Beckworth was rumored to rule over the darker money that came into England, word was that Malum controlled a good deal of the legitimate wealth. As well as most of what existed in-between.

Despite Malum's status and resources, most of the *ton* publicly shunned him. Behind closed doors, however, England's revered nobility proved their hypocrisy by patronizing the emporium on a regular basis.

All that aside, Reed was dubiously honored to find himself in the company of such men. And suddenly wary as hell.

Sighing internally, Reed resigned himself to yet more trouble. Had he inherited yet further debt, the kind that put him in trouble with the underbelly of society? He wouldn't exactly be surprised if that was the case. He turned to Westcott with a raised brow, and his friend chuckled.

"Have a seat." West shook a wayward lock of hair out of his eyes, crossed his feet, and slouched against the wall. "You're wondering why I asked you here."

Not fooled by West's friendly manner, Reed remained standing. "I'll admit to some curiosity," he conceded.

Helton leaned forward. "I'll skip the small talk, Rutherford—"

"Standish," Malum grunted, not looking up.

"Standish… Damn. Never thought I'd see the day," West inserted. "Anyhow, good to see you and all that, but I've asked you here because of the latest rumors."

"Rumors?" Reed cocked a brow. How many times had the two of them mocked some rumor or another?

West winced. "Unfortunately, yes. Talk that you murdered your predecessors is… gaining traction." Reed's friend's tone turned serious. "You need to put them down."

Reed frowned. "But they are only rumors."

"Rumors alleging murder," West pointed out. Before Reed could emphatically declare his innocence, West held up a hand. "I know they're false, but in society, even the most unfounded of suspicions take on a life of their own."

His friend, *the Piccadilly Player*, ought to know.

"Innocent or not, you're going to need help, Standish." Winterhope folded his arms across his chest, looking far too serious. "And if these dangerous rumors aren't subdued, the authorities will have no choice but to get involved."

Reed clutched his hands behind his back, stunned by this conversation.

"That's why you sent for me?" A moment ago, he would have laughed at this. But this powerful group of gentlemen most definitely were not laughing. And West had never been one to exaggerate or worry needlessly over anything.

Quite the opposite, actually.

"You need to put them to rest. Something you can't accomplish while hiding away at Rutherford Place." His old friend's tone remained somber.

"I thought peers were above accountability," Reed argued. Having managed both his father's and uncles' affairs for nearly a decade, he'd seen crime go unpunished often enough.

"But yours are unique circumstances," Winterhope said. "Because this crime, in particular, is against another peer—or in your case, peers."

"You could be thrown in Newgate," West said, "If these aren't squashed before the Season begins."

"The Season always complicates matters. There are more mouths to speculate. More ears to perk up to the gossip." Winterhope shrugged. "In general, more fuel."

The Season? But the first event of the Season was less than a fortnight away. *Bloody hell.*

"Surely it will die down as soon as some footman runs off with one of the new debutantes?" he offered.

"But we're talking about murder, Reed." West's voice was firm. "You simply cannot leave this to chance."

"And that's why West here asked for us to step in," Winterhope said. "Have a seat." He gestured toward a plush, high-backed chair.

"You'll want to take a look at this." Unsmiling, the Earl of Helton tossed a newspaper onto the small table in front of him.

Reed gingerly lowered himself onto the offered seat and shifted his gaze to the newspaper—which was, oddly enough, dated three days in the future. But it was the headline that sent his heart plummeting.

Tragic accident or murder—or worse?

"It's on everyone's minds. The public will demand a thorough investigation. It's impossible for me to ignore such a prominent scandal," Helton said. "But Westcott here says you were chums in school—mentioned that you'd helped him out a time or two. So, I'm willing to hold off. If you can change the narrative, give me something even more interesting by…" He glanced over to the fireplace, where a large clock sat upon the mantel. "Midnight Tuesday, I'll print this instead."

He tossed out a second paper.

"Standish marries the Duke of Crossings' daughter?" Reed asked. "But she was my cousin's fiancée." A bark of ironic laughter escaped. Even given an entire year, he doubted he could make the headline true.

As her fiancé's cousin, Reed had been introduced to Lady Gardenia Hathaway and even attended the house party to celebrate her and Rupert's betrothal. But it had been well known that he was there as a courtesy, and worked for his family as the estate manager. The duke's beautiful daughter had been polite enough but otherwise dismissive.

In truth, she'd been raised to be a duchess. Her mother had, in fact, made it clear that she'd considered even Rupert, heir to an earl, to be beneath her daughter. If not for Reed's uncle's dealings with the Duke of Crossings, the betrothal would never have come about.

"But you are Standish now," West pointed out.

Reed stared across the room at Helton, earl and publisher. "Couldn't you simply water down the first version?"

"No." Helton didn't even think about it. "Not if I'm going to make this paper profitable. But if you provide me with something to distract them…" He shrugged.

Reed swallowed, imagining a noose being dropped around his neck.

In exchange for one story, Helton wanted another. And it would have to be marriage. An exclusive announcement of a mere engagement to Crossings' daughter, while interesting, couldn't replace the drama of the first headline.

The first story was by far more damning. Words such as suicide, arson, murder, and even treason were all mentioned. The article would erase any hope he had for securing his sisters' futures. And if he did end up in Newgate, they'd be left to fend for themselves.

Newgate.

The word pinged around his brain and sweat snaked down his spine as he imagined walls closing in around him.

"You certainly are thorough." He grimaced.

"Not me," Helton said. "My reporters."

Reed shifted his attention to the second headline and exhaled. "You'll kill the first story if I convince Crossings' daughter to marry me before you go to print Tuesday night." Today was Sunday, and the day was already half over. So he'd have less than three days. The only way he saw himself succeeding in this demand was if he kidnapped the chit.

And that scenario had the potential to bring his standing even lower.

"It would hardly be worthy of the front page if you observed proper mourning first," Helton spoke around the cheroot in his mouth.

Reed shifted his gaze to West and then around the room before allowing it to land on Helton. He couldn't technically call this blackmail, but his arm might as well be twisting right out of the socket.

"Why?" Reed asked. "Why even give me a choice?"

Westcott's grimace turned into a deep frown. "Back at school, you came to my aid more than once. I'd do more if I could. But the rumors need to be squashed. I wouldn't have requested this meeting if it wasn't dire."

If the truth behind the fire were made public, his sisters could say goodbye to the possibility of landing proper husbands. Caroline, the eldest and most independent, would no doubt manage, but Melanie had always wanted a family, and Josephine had grown up with stars in her eyes. She was too young to have them extinguished.

And Reed… well, he wasn't sure how long he could survive being locked up in Newgate.

Contemplating the aftermath of the fire objectively, even Reed comprehended how the circumstances were damning.

But they were just that—circumstances.

Westcott reached into his pocket and pulled out a folded slip of parchment. "We've acquired a special license for you. Send word once you've secured her agreement and we'll make arrangements for a ceremony at St. George's on Tuesday evening—that way, I'll send word to Helton before he puts the paper to bed."

The location was simple enough—just across the square from Rutherford Place. But getting a bride there. That was a near impossibility.

Reed shook his head, imagining his cousin's former fiancée—the diamond of the Season, in fact. With her perfect figure, golden hair, and crystal blue eyes, Lady Gardenia could have anyone she wanted. "She'll never agree to it." She had a reputation for being her father's puppet, dancing to his tune, obeying the duke's every command. "There has to be another way."

"Nothing as newsworthy," Helton said. "Crossings' chit has been said to have the character of an angel. If she marries you, that's as good of a declaration of your innocence as you can hope for."

"You are Standish." The Duke of Malum pinned his gaze on Reed.

Ten minutes later, Reed marched past the towering cathedral on his way back to Rutherford Place on Hanover Square, one of the premier addresses in Mayfair.

Where he, Reed Rutherford, was lord of the manor now—a manor tended to by servants his uncle had employed. This was madness.

He rubbed the back of his neck.

But if he was going to bring honor back to the title and pave the way for his sisters' futures, he needed legitimacy.

If he wanted to maintain his freedom, he needed to squash all speculation. He wanted to be angry with Helton, but the blasted publisher was, in fact, offering him a bone.

Reed had no choice but to convince the duke's daughter to marry him.

SUNDAY AFTERNOON

❦

Goldie halted before opening the door to the drawing room, smoothed her gown over her rounder-than-fashionable hips, and then tucked a wayward curl behind her ear.

A curl on the opposite side fell forward, and she brushed that one back, but then the other escaped again.

"Blast!" She gave up on the endeavor entirely, and even as she shifted her bodice so as to cover more of her ample bosom, more curls escaped her coiffure.

Unlike her older sister, Goldie was graceless, awkward, and… hopeless.

But she wouldn't dwell on any of that now. She wouldn't because the man she admired most was here.

Today.

This very second.

Mr. Reed Rutherford, the new Earl of Standish. If she'd known he was coming, she'd have tried harder to make her hair behave.

She held her breath, anticipating a glimpse of his eyes, which were the exact color of bluebells in spring. They had been the first thing she'd noticed when she'd been introduced last summer at the house party to celebrate her sister's and Lord Rupert's betrothal. It hadn't mattered that he'd not noticed her.

She had not been meant to be noticed.

As a plump girl of ten and eight, she'd not come out yet but had been allowed to join the party for dinner. She'd been given strict instructions to keep quiet, however, and not make a nuisance of herself.

And she'd been perfectly fine with that most evenings because she'd usually been seated near Mr. Rutherford. She had been thoroughly pleased to simply watch his hands as he ate and listen to the rumble of his voice when he spoke.

His remarks had consistently been quiet and thoughtful, and unlike most of the other gentlemen, he'd never come across as boastful or arrogant.

Intelligence lurked behind his eyes, and he had spoken of his two dogs with great affection. His lack of refinement, rather than diminishing his attractiveness, had enhanced it.

His cousin, Lord Rupert, however, had been quite the opposite. His eyes had been hard and cold, and Goldie had failed to find any redeeming qualities in her sister's betrothed.

Mr. Rutherford, Goldie suspected, would make a far better earl than Lord Rupert would have.

But with his cousin dead and with no further ties between their two families, why had he come here—to her father's house?

She'd know soon enough.

Goldie turned the handle and, after a deep breath, stepped inside.

The back of his head faced her, allowing her a brief moment to admire his wide shoulders, slim hips, and overall magnificent physique. And as he turned to greet her, his eyes lit up with anticipation.

But then dimmed the instant he saw that she was not the lady with whom he'd requested to meet.

"My lady—" he began.

Goldie stepped forward. "You were expecting my sister," she interrupted, willing herself to breathe normally. "I'm afraid you're to be disappointed."

"She will return soon?" His brows crinkled, but his expression was all politeness.

"She is in mourning, my lord." Goldie flicked her gaze to the black band on Lord Standish's arm as she uttered the lie. And then she added, "I am sorry for your loss. Won't you sit down?"

He glanced around the room as though contemplating making his excuses, but when Goldie settled herself on the loveseat, he had no choice but to sit as well.

Looking rather stiff, he took the chair facing her.

Goldie arranged her skirts, again wishing her bodice was a little looser. Or did she struggle for breath because of this man's presence?

She twisted her hands in her lap and forced her expression into one that she hoped looked sympathetic rather than adoring. Stifling a nervous giggle at the thought, Goldie bit her lip.

She would keep her dignity throughout this meeting. The poor man had recently suffered a horrid tragedy.

It didn't matter that she'd not been overly impressed with the four gentlemen who'd perished; they'd been his kin.

His father. His brother. His cousin and his uncle—the former earl. It really was unimaginable.

But Goldie had spent several hours mooning over this particular man last summer at the house party.

Even back then, knowing he was an estate manager, she'd found Mr. Reed Rutherford to be inordinately attractive. Now, dressed in attire fitting of his new station this morning, snug breeches, elegant coat, and perfectly tied cravat, he was simply…

Beautiful.

She couldn't help but notice how perfectly his waistcoat matched his eyes.

Even brighter than the bluebells.

She sighed.

But now he was here, seated before her. And, unfortunately, they'd been seated for nearly a minute in silence. Goldie resisted the urge to squirm.

Why did he need to talk to Nia?

"How are Miss Rutherford and your other sisters? And your mother?" she asked. He had three younger sisters, but she couldn't remember all their names. No doubt they would have remained in the country to fulfill a proper mourning period.

"She is Lady Caroline now." Lord Standish frowned as though answering her question required great concentration. "She, Lady Melanie, Lady Josephine, and my mother are as well as can be expected. They traveled with me to London, in fact."

Goldie blushed at her blunder. With Mr. Rutherford inheriting the title, all of their lives had changed. "But they cannot go out in public." Surely they didn't intend to participate in the Season?

"Because of the rumors?" he asked. Was that a hint of a snarl?

"Because they are in mourning," Goldie provided.

"Ah, yes," he answered vaguely before falling silent again.

Goldie glanced at the clock on the mantel. But where were her manners? "Would you care for tea?" she asked.

Her father would not appreciate her inviting this man to extend his stay, but she refused to be rude. And already, she had no doubt that Mr. Bulwark, the butler, would be chastised for allowing Goldie to even meet with him.

Alone, no less.

If her father had been at home, he'd have tossed Lord Standish out before he could set foot inside. Because there were, indeed, rumors—unmentionable ones.

But Lord Standish didn't seem interested in tea.

"Do you know where I can find Lady Gardenia?" He looked anxious.

"I do not," Goldie said. "I mean, I do, but I can't tell you where. My father sent her away to observe six weeks of mourning." Not to mourn, really, but to distance her from any possible scandal. "She'll return when the Season begins."

Goldie studied Lord Standish's chin, firm but with a small dimple in the center. She'd noticed it before. His dark brown hair needed trimming, and a shadow darkened his cheeks and clenched jaw.

She couldn't quite make out the curse he made under his breath.

"Is there something that I can help you with?" she asked.

Holding his hat in one hand, he ran his other through his hair.

Hair that was thick and springy and clean-looking. She doubted any pomade could keep it in place.

Lord Standish lifted his gaze to meet hers, his eyes pleading. "I need to speak with your sister most urgently. I promise, my lady, I mean no ill will."

Oh, but she knew this about him. And under any other circumstances, she'd sing like a canary.

Nonetheless, Goldie bit her tongue. "I wish I could help you." She'd spend a month locked in her chamber if she went against her father's wishes.

"Is this about Lord Rupert's ring? Do you need it back?" she asked.

It was likely locked in her father's safe, no doubt, to which Goldie had long ago memorized the combination. Was she willing to risk her father's wrath for this man? It wasn't as though her sister cared about it. Nia had resented it from the beginning, and she wasn't about to wear it with her fiancé dead.

This would be one way that Goldie could perhaps ease some of the earl's disappointment. Would he notice her then?

Would her father even realize the ring was missing?

But Lord Standish scowled. "It's been returned already." He seemed even more apathetic about the ring than he'd been about tea.

Goldie nervously watched as the earl rubbed his hands along his muscular thighs.

"Perhaps if you tell me what you need, I can help you," she said. Why was he so distraught?

With his cousin dead, did he wish to attempt to win her sister's hand for himself?

Her sister was *Lady Gardenia*, the Duke of Crossings' eldest daughter, and had also been the diamond of the Season last year. Upon a single glance, most men immediately fell madly in love with Nia. Why wouldn't this one?

The intensity of his stare made Goldie sit up straight.

"Can you tell me one thing?" His eyes implored her.

With him staring at her like that, Goldie nearly melted.

"Maybe…" she answered.

"Is she in London?"

Goldie rolled her lips together before answering.

"She is not."

"Curses." He lowered his chin and seemed to be staring at her breasts. Even though his eyes appeared unfocused, Goldie felt a blush seeping across her skin.

"I'm sorry," she uttered.

After a few seconds, he exhaled a long hissing breath and met her gaze again. "My apologies."

And then he burst to his feet.

"I truly am sorry…" Goldie rose more slowly. She hated to see him looking so frustrated.

She hated that *she'd* been the one to disappoint him.

But he turned to her and bowed. "My thanks for receiving me."

And as quickly as he'd come, the Earl of Standish took his leave.

This was most serendipitous because not two minutes following his departure, the door to the drawing room was thrown open.

"What did that devil want?" Her father's ruddy complexion appeared even more red than usual, and his mere aura filled the room with tension.

Lord Standish was *not* a devil, but Goldie kept her opinion to herself.

"He wanted to see Gardenia." Her voice trembled more than she'd like.

Her father's long strides ate up the space between them. Most dukes possessed tremendous power and could intimidate a person without speaking. Her father, with his stout physique and permanent glower, intimidated even those who didn't know his status.

"Why didn't you tell Bulwark to send him away?" He pinned her to her seat with nothing more than his stare, and Goldie made herself as small as possible. Her father was not above striking his daughters.

"I didn't think. I'm sorry," she said.

"If that murderer steps foot in my house again, he'll be carried out by an undertaker."

But Lord Standish was *not* a murderer! Goldie didn't believe the stupid rumors for an instant. She wanted to tell her father that there was no evidence supporting those suspicions and that Lord Standish was nothing like the other men in his family.

But, of course, she could not.

"You never do." Her father's jaw ticked, but he kept silent as he strode across to the window. "Insults to humanity—the Rutherford men. The entire line ought to have ended in that fire. I was a fool to agree to the betrothal. I've made a lucky escape. Liars and cheats—the whole lot of them."

It was Nia who had made the lucky escape.

But Goldie didn't argue with her father—no one ever argued with the Duke of Crossings.

Those who did always regretted it.

"He won't be coming around again," she said. "I told him Gardenia was not in London."

Her father turned around. "I don't know what I did for God to curse me so. I'd trade both my daughters for a single son," he said. "At least I don't have to worry about any of these nobs coming after you. I can only console myself that your mother will have you as her companion once your sister is married."

"Unless my come-out is a success," Goldie reminded him in a timid voice, staring down at her hands. If she failed to land a husband this Season, she doubted she'd get another chance.

She loved her mother. She did! But the duchess could be picky and criticizing at times. Goldie couldn't picture herself tending to her every whim—not for the rest of her life!

Her father merely grunted.

"Mother promised they would return before the Season begins." Because Goldie required her mother's sponsorship if she was to be presented.

"I suppose, but you know how she is." He walked across the room but turned around when he arrived at the door. "Tell Bulwark that if he allows anyone with so much as an ounce of Rutherford blood to set foot in my house again, he's sacked. And if Standish persists in sniffing around you, hoping to get to your sister, inform me immediately and I'll demand satisfaction."

Goldie swallowed hard but nodded. Of course, she'd make sure the butler heeded her father's instructions. No matter how enamored she was with Lord Standish, she wouldn't allow Bulwark to lose his job.

She needed to forget about Lord Standish completely. He was nothing more than a childish crush.

A crush who was only interested in her sister.

Goldie straightened her spine. She had her come-out to look forward to.

She prayed she'd land a kind, quiet gentleman for a husband this Season. Love wasn't in her future, but freedom…

That was within her reach.

Even if she had to let go of Reed Rutherford to have it.

A LOOPHOLE?

If the hour had been earlier, Reed would have worked off his frustrations by taking his horse for a brisk ride on Rotten Row. Unfortunately, it was nearly the driving hour, and even in the off-season, he'd have to negotiate a few pedestrians.

His mind searching frantically for some other plan to save his family's reputation, he marched unseeing along Hanover Street until he arrived at Rutherford Place. Had West been exaggerating? But no, before allowing himself to contemplate the possibility, Reed dismissed it as wishful thinking.

He needed to discover where Crossings had sent Lady Gardenia. Get there, and convince her to return with him—as his fiancée. All within about fifty or so hours.

The instant he stepped inside the majestic foyer, a flurry of black appeared as the eldest of his younger sisters all but accosted him. "What did she say?" she asked.

Growing up, he'd been closer to Caroline than either Melanie or Josephine. At three and twenty, Caroline was only five years younger, whereas his other two sisters were nearly a full decade behind him.

Which was the only reason he'd shared the dire nature of their circumstances with her after returning from his meeting at the Emporium.

Aside from making the journey from their father's estate, Breaker's Cottage, to London, his mother and younger sisters had chosen to observe strict mourning. And although Reed was fairly certain his mother suspected the rumors, troubling her with the complications would serve no purpose.

Mr. Beasley, his butler now, appeared as though out of nowhere. Reed handed over his hat and coat but didn't answer Caroline's question until the door to the drawing room was closed behind them.

"Well?" Caroline demanded.

"Lady Gardenia is not in London." He dropped onto the settee and ran both hands through his hair.

"Did the duke's butler tell you that, or were you allowed to meet with the duke himself?" Caroline lowered herself as well but lifted her feet onto the settee and hugged her knees.

"He allowed me to meet with Lady Marigold." For an instant, Reed had believed his luck had changed. But then the younger sister had stood at the door.

And he'd been disappointed, to say the least.

And yet some carnal part of his person questioned how he'd not noticed this chit before.

With lush curves and rebellious blond curls, she presented herself as a tempting armful and quite worthy of notice. Even disregarding her more prominent attributes, one couldn't help but find her facial features just as noticeable: curious eyes, full lips, and skin that reminded him of honey and cream.

"She's a sweet girl," Caroline said. "Quiet, though."

"Well, she was too quiet for my purposes today."

"But she told you Lady Gardenia had left London. What else did she say?"

Reed searched his memory for tidbits from the brief meeting. Mostly, he'd been devastated to learn that Lady Gardenia was no longer in town. "I don't know."

"Where is she?" Caroline pressed.

"Lady Marigold?"

"No, dear brother." His sister sent her gaze rolling toward the ceiling. "Lady *Gardenia*."

"Lady Marigold refused to tell me."

"But she knows."

Reed tugged at the back of his neck. "Yes, but knowing Crossings, she'd suffer dire consequences if she were to tell me." He'd wanted to press Lady Marigold for more information but that wouldn't have been fair. If he pressed anyone, he'd press the goddamn Duke of Crossings himself.

"She would have told you if she could. Goldie's nothing like the rest of her family. And besides…" Caroline smiled.

Caroline's good humor made no sense at all, considering their predicament.

"Besides what?" Reed asked, irritated.

"She's head over heels for you." Caroline grinned. "At least she was last summer."

"Don't be ridiculous."

"Why am I not surprised you didn't notice?"

Reed pursed his lips. What the devil was his sister talking about? "Be serious."

"At the house party? She practically followed you everywhere," Caroline prompted.

Reed had attended his cousin's engagement celebration reluctantly and kept himself busy with correspondence most of the time. He vaguely remembered that the younger sister had been allowed to attend formal dinners.

She'd hardly spoken a word, dressed in an abundance of pastels and pink and an obnoxious amount of lace. She had seemed very, very young.

But she'd changed over the course of the past ten months.

"She rarely let you out of her sight." Caroline shook her head. "I almost felt sorry for her and would have, if she didn't exhibit such good taste."

"Ha," Reed responded, shaking his head at his sister's compliment. Because of course she would say that. "But I don't see how this has anything to do with me marrying her sister."

"Did she flirt with you while you were there today?"

"What? Not at all." But she had been sweet. She'd treated him with almost lavish politeness. "She was rather kind, actually." She'd asked him to stay for tea, but he'd ignored the invitation.

In fact, she'd been more than willing to listen to his troubles.

And he'd been…

Distracted by the devastating blow she'd served up.

Caroline sat very still but Reed could practically hear her brain as it began devising some scheme.

"That newspaper man…" she began.

"Lord Helton." Reed narrowed his eyes.

"He said you must marry Crossings' daughter, yes?"

"Yes."

"Did he specifically say that you needed to wed Lady *Gardenia*?"

Reed recalled the meeting he'd had at the *Domus Emporium* the day before. "Her name was the one mentioned in the article."

"But when saying you must marry Crossings' daughter, did he say Lady Gardenia specifically?"

Reed scowled. They had not. But still—

"Do you have the special license with you?"

Reed had, in fact, optimistically brought it with him to the duke's townhouse. Oh, how misguided he'd been to even entertain the thought that his quest would be fulfilled so easily. He pulled it out of his jacket and handed it to his sister.

Reading it, she bit her lip and then met his gaze.

"The name of the bride is blank." Caroline sounded far too cunning. The same as whenever she plotted some ill-fated scheme.

"Surely you aren't suggesting…?"

"Lady Marigold is the duke's daughter. And marrying her, although not as scandalous as if you were to marry her sister, would be almost as interesting to the Gazette's readers…"

"He meant Lady Gardenia," Reed said.

"But he only said the Duke of Crossings' daughter. Do you think he'll honor his agreement so long as you give him a good story?"

Helton, an earl, likely would. "It wouldn't be honorable on my part," Reed pointed out. "There has to be some other way."

Caroline leaned back, squeezing her knees nearly to her chin. "Unless Lady Gardenia makes an unlikely appearance, Reed, we're stumped."

"There has to be something," he insisted.

"Well," Caroline held his gaze. "It's not as though any of us have bosom buddies here in Mayfair who can tell us where Lady Gardenia is. Even if we did, we're supposed to be in mourning. And the rumor needs squashed. West and that publisher fellow don't seem the sort to exaggerate something like this. They've spent far more time in town than any of us, and no doubt understand better how these matters play out."

Reed huffed. He hated when his sister made sense.

"And," Caroline continued. "With plan 'A' having failed, plan 'B' is your only choice. I don't want to see you in Newgate, brother." Her sad smile tugged at Reed's heart.

"Plan 'B,' I take it, being Lady Marigold?" He couldn't believe he was contemplating this. "You really think she'll be willing to help me?"

"More than that, I think she'll be thrilled to marry you. Simply ask her. With Lady Gardenia on the marriage mart again this spring, and a father like the Duke of Crossings, the poor girl lacks options."

Reed frowned as he considered the young woman he'd met with earlier that morning. She'd been sweet and pretty and…

Lush.

"I don't know why you'd say she lacks options."

"She's pretty enough," Caroline conceded. "But on all other counts, she pales in comparison to her sister."

"How so?" Women baffled him at times.

"She's the second daughter. And lacking her sister's beauty and refinement, I'd wager a year's allowance that all her future holds is a lifetime catering to her mother." Caroline cocked a brow. "You do remember the duchess, don't you?"

Reed did, in fact, recall how demanding the woman was.

"Poor Lady Marigold simply isn't… marriage material. I like her. She's intelligent. But she is just not at all a typical debutante."

Which, Reed thought, was the highest of compliments.

Damn, Caroline could almost convince him that he'd be doing the poor girl a favor.

"If I can't get information on Lady Gardenia's whereabouts, I'll run the idea past West," he said. "Tomorrow."

"It's not as though you have many other options, Reed." Caroline shrugged. "Or much time. Besides, it'll be easy. Trust me."

MONDAY

After a restless night's sleep, with the sun not quite yet risen, Reed knew the best place to find his friend would be on Rotten Row. He was not disappointed.

By the time he arrived at the park, familiar faces, along with a handful of other gents, were already racing up and down the Row. West was on the largest stallion of them all.

After sprinting past Reed on his giant of a horse, West then pulled the powerful animal to a halt and turned to walk back.

Reed waved as his old friend approached. "Where'd you find this extraordinary animal?" Reed studied Westcliff's mount, who stood at least two hands higher than his own. "Impressive," he said.

"This is Bard, one of the latest from Winterhope's stables."

"If the marquess has others like this one, his stables must be as good as they're rumored to be."

Reed appreciated discussing something—anything—other than his current troubles. But he only allowed himself a few minutes.

He couldn't very well go forward with Caroline's plan

without West's support because West would be at the wedding. He would be one of the witnesses.

Reed exhaled a breath, staring unseeing at the cresting sun.

"Lady Gardenia isn't in London," West stated, beating him to the punch.

"No." Of course, the *Piccadilly Player* would be privy to such information. "You don't know where I can find her, do you?"

Westcott sighed. "Word is that Crossings has sent her to his estate near Southampton. But she might only be as far as Bath. Regardless, it would be impossible for you to make the journey to and back from either in time to meet Helton's deadline."

"Hear me out." Reed rubbed the bridge of his nose before continuing. "Crossings has another daughter."

After a pause, Westcott snapped his head to stare over at him, his brow furrowed.

"What are you getting at?"

Reed couldn't tell if his friend was angry or intrigued.

"Lady Marigold is in town." Reed winced. "What are the chances of Helton accepting a minor twist to the story?"

His normally carefree-looking friend frowned but then turned thoughtful. "He did not, in fact, specify which daughter."

"Aside from the actual article," Reed pointed out.

"Yes, but… Don't tell me. This is Lady Caroline's idea?"

"How did you know?"

"She's more cunning than you are." West laughed.

"Yes, well." Ceres, Reed's mount, skittered beneath him, anxious for a well-deserved run. Reed ran a calming hand down her neck. "Any chance it'll work?"

West remained silent for almost a full thirty seconds. "He won't like it, but… Honestly, Rutherford, with Lady Gardenia in seclusion, you haven't much choice."

Exactly what he and Caroline had deduced.

It was all Reed needed to hear. At least he had a course of

action he could follow now—even if it wasn't the most honorable one.

Because he had others besides himself to consider.

"In that case." He leaned over Ceres. "I suppose I ought to change into something more appropriate." He couldn't exactly propose while smelling of horses.

"Send word when you've secured her hand. Along with the hour of the happy occasion." A joke, of course, because West made no bones regarding his personal disdain for the institution. "I'll stand up with you at St. George's." West laughed.

"Someday I'll return the favor," Reed threatened.

"Not if I can help it." West laughed. "But seriously, don't put this off too late."

Reed dipped his chin. Despite the unease in his shoulders, by God, he was going to do it. It was either that or…

Full-on catastrophe for himself and his mother and sisters.

With a quick wave, he loosened the rein in his hand and all but flew to the other end of the park.

~

Goldie slid her hands into her gloves and stepped outside. The sun shone brightly, but the air was crisp, so she walked swiftly in the direction of Bond Street. Her father rarely woke before noon, and so since coming to Mayfair, Goldie had learned that if she wanted any time to explore, she'd have to do it in the early hours.

Alone, she could breathe freely, smile only when she felt like it, and allow her posture to slump naturally. Furthermore, she wasn't constantly anticipating one of her father's outbursts.

On this particular morning, she'd decided to first purchase a handful of flowers from one of the morning vendors, and after that, she'd visit her favorite bookstore.

Perhaps after Nia and her mother returned, she could visit the menagerie or even purchase an ice from Gunter's.

Once Goldie became an official debutante, she could finally visit all the places Nia had told her about. Only her sister, of course, had been squired about by gentlemen vying for her hand.

What would that be like?

Lord Standish's image appeared unbidden in her mind, but instead of her usual fluttering heart, she felt…

Disappointment.

Like all the others, he'd come looking for Nia. The feelings she'd had for him last summer had been childish. He'd been kind to her, but not because he'd returned her affection. In truth, he'd barely noticed her, and now that he was an earl, he had even less reason to single her out.

This spring, she would find a mild-mannered landowner for a husband. In the first few years, she'd provide him an heir and a spare. Following that, they would pursue their separate interests while settling into a comfortable lifestyle.

She'd have to be careful in choosing such a man, however, as gentlemen were not incapable of hiding their true character.

Take Lord Rupert, for instance. A ghostly chill slid down Goldie's spine, making her shiver, but when she glanced around, she saw nothing out of the ordinary.

Nonetheless, she remained wary.

She wasn't, in fact, entirely comfortable going about without a chaperone. If she didn't know for a fact her outings would get back to her father, she would have brought one of the maids along. Goldie hadn't much choice.

She could either sit embroidering alone all day or summon her courage and go into the world alone.

And by "world," she meant the nearby narrow streets that encircled most of Mayfair.

Her tame idea of adventure made her chuckle. She had

nothing to fear. She tilted her head back with her eyes closed and briefly enjoyed the hint of warmth provided by the sun.

"Do share in your joke, my lady."

Goldie's eyes flew open, and she found herself staring at the man she'd just dismissed from her thoughts.

Or had tried to, anyhow. The same as she'd done numerous times since last summer.

For all the reasons she'd found him attractive and more, his sudden appearance stole her breath.

The tiny wrinkles around his eyes when he smiled, and a swagger that came from being fit and agile. Dear heavens, the low grumble in his voice had her imagining all manner of wicked scenarios.

No lady ought to ponder such ideas...

But yesterday, he had come asking about Nia—less than a month following the death of Nia's fiancé, *his cousin.*

"Simply enjoying the sunshine, my lord." Goldie tried to sound cold, despite allowing herself a second glance at his...

Glorious manliness.

She kept right on walking.

His attire was identical to what he'd worn the day before, but this morning he didn't seem nearly as distracted as he matched his strides to hers.

"Unusual for this time of year." He jammed his hands into his pockets. She wasn't all that far from her father's house. Had he come hoping she'd give the information she'd withheld the day before?

"I cannot tell you where she is, my lord." Goldie didn't want to fill in for her sister again. "I will not." She glanced behind her anxiously. If word got back to her father that she'd been walking with the new Earl of Standish, she'd suffer for it. "Is there anything else I can do for you?" She kept her face forward and increased her pace.

"Should you be out walking alone like this?"

"No." Goldie winced. "Nor should I be seen walking with you."

"And yet you are doing both?" There was a hint of laughter in his voice.

"You are not welcome in my father's house, my lord," she tried again.

"But I am not in his house, Lady Marigold." He kept pace right beside her. "So, technically…"

"I already told you, I can't tell you where my sister—"

"But I am not walking with your sister," he said. "I'm walking with you."

Goldie's feet stumbled to a halt, and not quite believing this was happening, she turned to glare up at him.

"Why?" How many times had she wished for this very scenario last summer? She ought to be ecstatic, and yet, it didn't make sense. Did he have some ulterior motive? Would she be a fool to trust his sudden interest in… *her*?

They'd been walking along the park, and, arriving at a path leading across the vast lawn, he gestured toward it. "It's a beautiful day. Stroll with me?"

And then he smiled.

Dash it all! This, his most potent weapon of all, must be her greatest weakness.

"Very well." She had no power against a smile like that. "But only along the wooded paths. I can't have this getting back to my father."

∼

R*eed offered his arm*, and Lady Marigold took it without a second of hesitation. Her hand felt small and warm even through his jacket, and when the breeze caught her hair, a hint of fruit teased his nostrils.

This innocent young woman smelled like strawberries.

"You are out early, by *Tonnish* standards." Her voice sounded breathless.

"But it's the early bird that gets the proverbial worm, is it not?"

"Are you implying that I'm a worm?" But she did not sound offended. In fact, she laughed again, and the alto tones of the sound sent a bewildering current vibrating through him.

"Perhaps I am the worm." He sent her a teasing glance.

"Oh, that's far more fitting." They entered a wooded area, and she trailed her gloved fingertips along leaves that sprouted low on some of the trees. "But what kind of bird am I?"

"A starling?" Reed played along. He'd expected flirting to be more difficult than this. And yet…

Flirting with Lady Marigold came with surprising ease.

"Hmm… I do like wild starlings," she said.

"What do you like about them?"

"A family of them made their home in the garden at Cross Castle. I think it's lovely how their feathers develop those little white spots in winter. And they are deceptively smart. I once caught a starling in our garden mimicking cricket sounds. I don't think they do that by accident." She drew her hand away from the trees and raised it to her chin thoughtfully. "I wouldn't mind being a starling… What kind of bird would you be?"

"But I'm the worm."

"An earthworm," she giggled.

Reed laughed and then feigned a shudder. "Oh, hell. I'd be a meal then. I suppose I would prefer to be a bird."

"Not a blue jay," she declared.

"And why would you say that?"

"Blue jays are bullies. They demand to be first. They don't like to share…"

"Hmmm…" Reed wondered if she was imagining her father.

"I've met my fair share of bullies, I must admit. I hope you have not."

"Only a few…" And then she blushed. Of course, she wasn't thinking of members of her family, but of his.

"No need to hold back. I am well aware of Rupert's failures." And those of his father, his uncle, and his brother. "But comparing them isn't fair to the bird."

She looked horrified but then, after a short pause, laughed and covered her mouth. "I'm sorry."

"No, I'm sorry." And to keep the conversation light, Reed said, "I actually feel an affinity with crows."

"Crows?"

Reed glanced down, expecting her to protest. Most people viewed crows to be opportunistic. Instead, she was nodding.

"I can see that," she said. "Crows are quite clever, really. And practical."

He appreciated their sleek watchfulness, but hadn't considered other characteristics.

But she wasn't finished. "They make use of what resources are available to them. They are problem solvers and very protective of what is theirs. Like you."

Caroline had said Lady Marigold had watched him closely at the house party. And he'd… well.

He'd dismissed her as a child. But she had seen things about him that few others ever had.

"I'm flattered." He would not embarrass her for having watched him. She was an innocent—caught up in his less-than-honorable scheme. She deserved better.

Reed exhaled. "I'm afraid I have a confession."

She stiffened and ducked her head, disappointment rolling off her. "Of course…" She erupted with a cynical laugh—a sound too bitter to come from such an innocent. "I should have realized."

But Reed cleared his throat and charged forward. "I came looking for you today," he said.

"Why?" She whipped around to stare at him. "Why would *you* come looking for *me*?"

He could compliment her looks, buy her presents and flowers. But that wasn't the way he operated. When he needed something, he first tried the most straightforward means of acquiring it.

"To ask you to marry me."

He didn't have a chance to check her expression because her foot caught on a root, and if he'd not been there to catch her, she would have slammed unceremoniously onto the packed dirt. Then again, if he'd not been there, she likely wouldn't have tripped at all.

Nonetheless, Reed caught her.

THE DETAILS

She didn't make it to the ground, but the breath whooshed out of her as though she had.

Surely, she'd heard incorrectly. He cannot have actually proposed.

To her, of all people!

"What? I mean, pardon?" She struggled to catch her breath as sturdy hands grasped her waist. The two of them had come to a halt, surrounded by trees and brush with the sky hidden by a giant canopy of branches and leaves.

"I'd like to marry you. Hell, I don't suppose that's the proper way of going about this sort of thing." He released her and then removed his hat to rake his fingers through his hair.

"But… Why?" Goldie glanced around them to see if there might be a collection of witnesses taking part in some sort of joke.

But there was no one. And when her gaze landed on Lord Standish once again, his expression appeared genuine.

"I need… I need a wife," he answered.

"Does this have something to do with the rumors?"

He winced. "You know, then."

"Only from my father. I've not yet had the opportunity to make friends here in London. I wouldn't expect that you'd remember me telling you last summer that I'm going to make my come-out this year."

He stared at her. "I do, actually. Are you excited about that?"

Two days ago, Goldie would have answered emphatically that yes, she was. But now... She resumed walking, and he matched his much longer strides to hers.

"I'd like to marry," she mused as she tried to picture some faceless, mild-mannered gentleman offering for her after obtaining her father's permission.

But the man beside her thoroughly monopolized all her brain space.

"Is that a yes, then?" He glanced sideways, cocking a brow.

A hopeful glance?

She'd not said yes because her father would never allow it. This was everything she'd ever wanted and all that she could not have, a fantasy that she'd finally accepted as such, and it made no sense that he would come to her now, presenting it as a potential reality when she was the same person she'd been last summer.

"But why me?" Goldie asked. This had to be a joke.

"Why *not* you?" The ground became even more uneven, and he casually took hold of her elbow. "You're refined and pretty. I can tell that you're intelligent. You'd make a lovely countess."

"As would any other debutante coming to London this spring," Goldie insisted. "Besides, you don't even know me."

"I know you are an excellent listener. I think you are quite brave and perhaps a little foolish to walk about London without a chaperone." They were nearing the clearing, and he stopped and turned her to face him. "I would be forever grateful if you would accept."

But...

But.

Goldie resisted the urge to pinch herself. This was not a dream, and yet… this was ridiculous! "My father would never agree to it."

The earl's expression turned sheepish. "No, he wouldn't, my lady."

Never in a million years would she have imagined having this conversation.

Was it possible that when he'd come to her father's house the day before, he'd fallen in love with her? Goldie dismissed the notion the instant she conjured it up.

He cannot have. He'd barely noticed her.

But had he realized he was attracted to her?

Goldie blinked, staring into his beautiful blue eyes. "You might as well call me Goldie." Her voice came out hoarse-sounding, and heat blossomed in her heart when she noticed him staring at her mouth.

"Goldie." Nothing else. And then, without warning, he leaned closer and touched his mouth to hers.

She'd once asked Nia what it felt like to be kissed. Her sister had grimaced, saying it wasn't horrible so long as the person kissing you hadn't recently consumed onions or garlic or any other unsavory food.

But Goldie had suspected there was more to kissing than that.

She had been right.

His lips were the perfect amount of soft and hard, and his taste was minty and spicy and something foreign and delicious.

He teased the seam of her mouth with his tongue, and she only resisted for a second before parting her lips. And as though she'd been kissing men all her life, she slid her hands onto his chest--to keep her balance, but also to assure herself this was real.

He was hard, and beneath her palms, she could feel the beating of his heart.

Vibrations of warmth and excitement coursed through her. She lost all sense of time—all sense of anything but of him and of her.

It was as though all her dreams manifested in this single moment.

It ought to have been a dream. But it wasn't.

His arms drew her closer, but with a groan, Lord Standish loosened his hold and suspended the kiss.

"I didn't... I'm sorry." He bent his head forward, resting his forehead on hers. "I didn't mean to do that." He sounded almost as surprised as she felt.

Not that a kiss wasn't the perfect accompaniment to a marriage proposal, but they had moved from being casual acquaintances to a courting couple over the course of two minutes.

It could not be real.

This... could not be real.

"You kissed me." Goldie stared at the backs of her gloved hands, which rested on the wool of his coat. This close, she could practically count the whiskers on his chin and jaw. She could study the pink of his lips, dewy wet from kissing her.

His chuckle rumbled through her entire body.

"Yes, I suppose I did," he said.

And then he tipped her chin back and stared into her eyes. "Will you? Will you marry me?"

Goldie rolled her lips together. She wanted this to be real. She wanted to believe he'd suddenly been overwhelmed with his attraction for her, but...

Something was off.

She shook her head. "I'll think about it."

An expression flashed across his face—disappointment?

But he dropped his hands from her waist, and when he took a step back, Goldie's hands slid off his chest.

Cold chased away the warmth from a moment earlier.

"I need an answer right away." He stared over her shoulder as though lost in thought. "I realize the timeline is unprecedented…"

"How soon?" Goldie asked and then swallowed hard. "How soon do you need to know?"

Most of her yearned to accept—particularly her heart, her mouth, her arms—good heavens, even the aching in her breasts and between her legs!

This was an opportunity to marry the object of her most heartfelt affection, for heaven's sake! But it was her head that kept her from accepting him outright—a decision-making part of her that was solid and familiar.

"I'll need your answer by tomorrow afternoon."

"You cannot be serious." Why was he in such a hurry? Gone was the man who'd held her so tenderly moments before. This man…

Was quite determined.

He dipped his chin.

"But I hardly know you," she protested. Yes, she'd put herself in his path whenever possible last summer. But the man she'd mooned over had been fifth in line to an earldom—he'd been a steward of the earl's properties. And now.

Now he was the earl.

Surely, taking on such a responsibility could change a person. Had they changed him?

Furthermore, as Standish now, he could have his pick of the debutantes this season.

Although the rumors were rather alarming. Goldie narrowed her eyes. Her own father had ordered her to keep away from him. Were the rumors bad enough so as to make him unmarriageable?

Surely not!

"You know next to nothing about me," she added.

"True." He studied her, rubbing his chin thoughtfully.

"Would you come out with me later this afternoon? Are you up for an adventure?"

A single outing would not be long enough that she could agree to his proposal, but an adventure…

It was just the sort of escape she craved!

And perhaps after spending a few hours alone in his company, he would become a real person to her. As the earl, he might even reveal a few warts, so to speak. And she could put him out of her mind once and for all.

But to leave the house in the afternoon, she'd have to make up some excuse to give her father.

"I won't change my mind," she said. It was only fair to be upfront with him. "If you need to marry quickly, you'll be wasting your time with me."

"I'll be the judge of that." He pinned his gorgeous blue eyes on her. "Because I want *you*."

Ecstatic bubbles burst from Goldie's heart and traveled outward to her fingertips and toes.

And her knees nearly buckled.

He wanted her!

She nodded. "Very well, then. I'll meet you this afternoon—at the entrance to the park.

"At three?" he asked.

"At three."

COURTSHIP

*A*fter handing his coat and hat off to Mr. Beasley, Reed stepped into the drawing room, knowing his sister would be anxiously waiting to hear of any progress he'd made.

"Were you able to meet with her?" Caroline burst off the settee, pushing loose strands of dark hair behind her ears. It was something Lady Marigold did, but whereas Caroline's hair was brown and straight, Goldie's was blond and curly.

"What did she say?" Caroline prodded.

Two questions, both of which the answers were more complicated than he'd imagined they would be.

"Well," Reed began. "In answer to your first question, yes. In answer to the second, she did not say 'no.'"

Caroline's eyes widened, so he added, "Nor did she say 'yes.'"

Lady Marigold ought to have—for her own sake. What the devil had gotten into him? Kissing her like that? He'd been standing there, contemplating the color of her eyes, a swirling myriad of browns and golds and greens, and then, without consciously deciding to do so, he'd pulled her into his arms and tasted luscious raspberry lips.

"But it might work." His sister dropped into her seat again, slouching this time, no doubt relieved that Lady Marigold had not sent him packing.

"I'm taking her driving this afternoon," Reed said, inexplicably remembering how she'd fit in his arms—soft, yielding. Holding her against his body like that had been something of a revelation.

He'd been aroused, he'd not deny that, but he'd also felt interest—attraction.

The cacophony of emotions had been raw, and more than he'd felt in months.

"You can use the curricle Rupert purchased last spring. It's quite spectacular—bright red. You'd be surprised at how impressive a fancy vehicle can be," Caroline said. "And you must bring her flowers."

Flowers, yes. But his chest tightened at the thought of taking out Rupert's ridiculously flamboyant high-flyer. Once he'd sorted through the current mess that was his life, he'd sell the damn thing and replace it with something more practical.

But Caroline had latched onto the idea. "Rand took me driving in it once—while Rupert was…ill. Perched so high like that, above every other vehicle, made me feel like the queen herself," his sister said. "Even Randal could be charming when he put his mind to it."

"When he wasn't out of his mind," Reed added, cutting off an inappropriate expletive. Both his brother and his cousin could have been so much more, if only…

"It's all right to miss them, you know," Caroline spoke softly.

But Reed wouldn't waste his time or energy there. All four men had made their choices—stupid, horrific choices—and left Reed to clean up after them.

His jaw clenched. He had other worries. Worries that

involved family members who depended on him—members who'd not chosen to live so recklessly.

Furthermore, dwelling on the past wasn't going to land him a duke's daughter for a wife. He had an afternoon to plan.

"I don't want to draw attention to the two of us. She's going to have to sneak out of her father's house as it is." He hated the cagey nature of this entire endeavor but was going to have to ignore his sensibilities until the rumors subsided. He could borrow West's curricle, but it, too, would draw attention.

Should he kiss her again? The first time had been… instinctive. But kissing her a second time could be considered strategic. And if he used romance and affection to convince her to marry him, what the hell sort of man did that make him?

Nothing to be proud of, that was for certain.

And yet, he wouldn't mind kissing her again.

"What is it?" Caroline, who had been watching him closely, asked.

"What do you mean?"

"That look on your face. What else happened this morning? You look… strange."

Reed scrubbed a hand down his face. *Blasted Caroline*. She'd pester him until he gave in. Although… Caroline, as a woman herself, might have some sort of insight into what Miss Goldie might be thinking about now.

Goldie. It was the perfect name for the blond bundle of sunshine.

"I kissed her," he admitted.

"Ah…" Her skeptical tone didn't provide the encouragement he'd hoped for. "Why did you kiss her, Reed? Because as badly as we need you to marry her, it wouldn't be fair to play with her affections like that." And then she frowned. "Would it?"

"Hell if I know. You were the one who pointed out that." Reed cleared his throat. "That she noticed me at the house party last summer." And damned if he didn't feel heat ebbing up his neck.

"True." Caroline seemed to come to some decision. "You can flirt and a kiss or two might be acceptable, but you absolutely cannot seduce her into accepting."

He turned and faced his sister in astonishment. "What do you know about seduction?"

She shrugged. "Enough to know it wouldn't be fair play on your part."

"Of course it wouldn't be," Reed grumbled.

"I can't believe you actually kissed her." Caroline frowned, but only for a moment, before her face lit up with understanding. "Oh, Reed. You like her, don't you? Of course, you're not the sort of man who would prey upon a woman's feelings like that. You like her!"

"She's a pleasant enough young woman," Reed conceded.

"But you like her! You. Like. Her!" Caroline seemed almost giddy over this. "Your marriage doesn't have to be a cold business arrangement." She clasped her hands together. "It could very well turn into a love match! And there will be children! Of course, I shall be their favorite aunt."

Marriage.

Reed's stomach lurched.

As a steward, Reed had never considered the institution for himself. And yet, he'd proposed to a young woman this very morning. And Caroline, by God, was mentioning children now.

A wedding ceremony was one thing—half an hour, give or take a few minutes—but a marriage…

It was for life. All the blood he'd felt in his face a few seconds earlier surely had drained away, and his chest seemed to collapse as he considered all the implications of marrying Lady Marigold.

"Reed," Caroline moved to sit beside him and touched his arm.

He turned to face his sister.

"You need to do everything possible to convince her. If you happen to feel affection for her, I think that can only be a good thing. But you haven't much choice. I refuse to allow you to be carted off to Newgate."

Reed was none too fond of the prospect himself.

"We'll be fine," he promised. "Trust me. We'll be fine."

THE FATHER

"*B*ulwark says you went walking this morning," the duke grumbled without looking up from the Gazette. He sat in his usual spot at the table, cigar smoke curling up from the small dish where it rested while he drank his tea.

"Yes. There's no one to run into when I go out early. Especially since the Season has yet to begin." Goldie deliberately kept her eyes focused on her knife as she spread marmalade on a warm piece of toast.

He kissed me!

Mr. Reed Rutherford had kissed her! *Lord Standish*! If Nia had been at home, Goldie would have gone straight to her. But Nia was gone.

And he'd said he wanted to marry her.

No one else. Just her. Marigold Hathaway! He'd not mentioned that she was too plump or that her hair curled more than was fashionable. And he'd not chided her for being clumsy when she'd nearly tripped over the tree root.

No. He'd said he wanted…

Her.

There must be a catch.

Which was why she'd not accepted his proposal. Well, it was one of the reasons she'd not accepted. The little matter of her father's disapproval, to put it lightly, was another one. Oh, but her father would kill the new earl if he knew of their conversation in the park this morning.

And that kiss! Trickles of honey flowed around her heart.

Goldie would remember it forever. The way he'd smelled of soap and leather and… just himself. His chest, beneath her fingertips, had felt as firm as the earth. His heartbeat had thumped under her palm, racing nearly as quickly as her own.

Warm heat had spread through her entire body, making her want more.

Would he kiss her again this afternoon?

She exhaled a dreamy sigh.

"What are you mooning about over there?" Her father pinned stormy eyes on her.

"Oh," Goldie caught herself. "This marmalade is delightful." And it was. The strawberry flavor danced in her mouth as the butter brought her tastebuds to life.

"You have too great a fondness for sweets." He raised his brows meaningfully. Derisively. "But I don't suppose it matters," he added.

This was nothing new. Her mother had often made similar comments.

Nia never did. Nia had told her that although Goldie's figure wasn't fashionable, it was lovely. *Gorgeously curvy*, she'd said.

Nonetheless, Goldie dropped the toast onto her plate.

"I have an… er… fitting scheduled for this afternoon."

Her father's gaze fell on the paper once again as he shook his head. "Damned waste of money, your coming-out."

"But you promised…" Goldie sat up straight. "And it'll be worth it—just you wait."

"Harumph! I could put your dowry to far better use. Not to mention—"

Goldie wouldn't allow him to finish and abruptly pushed her chair back. "I'm going to write a letter to mother—and to Nia—reminding them that the first ball is in twelve days. And she needs to arrange an evening at Almacks. I can't exactly make my come-out without a sponsor."

A scoffing grunt followed her out the door. He'd promised, and she was going to hold him to it.

But for now, she had more pressing concerns. A glance at the clock reminded her that she only had a few hours until she was to go driving with Lord Standish.

Of course, she couldn't accept his offer. Her father would never forgive her. She'd be banished from their family forever—from her mother, and from Nia.

Even contemplating it felt like a betrayal.

And yet, when she went upstairs, she removed her favorite day gown from the wardrobe and smoothed it out with a damp cloth. While it hung to dry, Goldie then proceeded to put her hair up in a pretty knot.

Her cheeks were flushed, and her eyes lit with anticipation.

He had kissed her.

And he might just kiss her again.

AT PRECISELY THREE o'clock in the afternoon, wearing a pale indigo muslin with blue birds embroidered at the hem, her best gloves, and a pair of practical half-boots, Goldie stood waiting at the entrance of the park as agreed upon.

What if he didn't come? What if it had all been a joke?

But at three oh one, a hackney pulled up beside her and the earl jumped out. He looked as relieved to see her as she was to see him.

He held out a hand. "Your chariot awaits, my lady."

It was not a tall gleaming curricle like the one Lord Rupert had squired Nia around in—nor was it even a handsome open barouche. It was a dull black carriage for hire.

Tamping down her disappointment, she nodded and allowed him to assist her inside.

And his touch immediately swept that disappointment away. With sturdy hands, he offered support while she maneuvered the step. Once she was seated, he gracefully hopped in and took the seat beside her.

"I considered one of my cousin's or uncle's vehicles," he said, staring straight ahead as the driver rejoined traffic. "But I didn't think you'd want to be recognized."

How careless of her not to have considered that! She'd foolishly been imagining the outing to be a proper one. But there was nothing proper about it in the least.

Not when she'd had to lie to her father about where she would be that day. Any of the Standish vehicles would be easily recognized driving around town. She ought to have considered that but had been too caught up in her excitement. Apparently, she was more naïve than she'd realized.

And he'd guessed her doubts immediately!

"Thank you," Goldie answered. She glanced down at her hands, where she'd managed to pull off one of her gloves and twist it into a mangled mess. But if they couldn't risk being seen together, that would eliminate all the usual places gentlemen took ladies while courting them. "What kind of an adventure are you taking me on?"

His glance landed on her gloves, but rather than comment on her nervousness, he said, "Have you ever been to one of the traveling fairs that come through London?"

A traveling fair? Her father would never allow it!

"I have not."

"Then you're in for a treat. And you look lovely, by the way. I should have told you that right off, shouldn't I? I'm not used to this sort of thing. But as I'm sure you know, London is full of gossips even in the off-season. I was mostly concerned with keeping you out of sight." He cleared his throat. "I've no wish to cause you any more trouble than necessary."

He sounded... contrite, so Goldie shifted to see his expression. "It was my choice to come." He'd not coerced her in any way.

Not unless one considered kissing a form of coercion. And if that was the case, she wouldn't mind being coerced a few more times...

He cleared his throat again. "The fairs are entertaining but also raucous. Easy to remain anonymous once you've joined the throngs, but if you're not comfortable with the idea, we can—"

"A fair sounds delightful!" But she glanced down at her gown. "Am I dressed properly, though?"

It wasn't the sort of question she'd normally ask a gentleman, and the instant his eyes trailed over her bodice, she realized why.

If his mere gaze could summon such heat, such... awareness, what would it feel like to be touched by him? To be his wife?

A moot question if ever there was one.

She *could* not accept him, so... Goldie bit her lip.

"You look perfect." His heated stare met hers before he quickly turned to face forward again.

But Goldie knew somehow that he, too, was remembering the kiss.

"It will be fun," she said, trying to keep their conversation cheerful. "To see parts of London where I'm not usually allowed." Her father could be quite tyrannical in regard to the freedoms he allowed his daughters. It was Nia, however, who was considered the beauty and most in need of protection.

"Indeed," Lord Standish said but then fell silent again.

"Have you been before?" Goldie asked before the pause could stretch on too long. "To the fair?" The silence made her uncomfortable. She felt the need to entertain him.

"A few times," he answered, and a hint of a smile danced on his lips. "When I was younger. It's an unlikely harmony of mismatched oddities, the vain, the garish, interspersed with an occasional display of nature's wonders."

"Not unlike the *Ton*," Goldie immediately made the connection and then covered her mouth. Because, as Standish, he was now an official member of society himself. As had been the men who'd died—as were his sisters and mother. "I'm sorry—"

But he interrupted her apology with a burst of laughter—the kind that lit up his eyes—the kind that made her happy that she'd amused him.

"Quite a lot like the *Ton*, I imagine," he said. "Although, I've yet to spend an entire season in Mayfair."

"Nor have I," Goldie admitted. "But I've heard things…"

"As have I." His eyes twinkled, and she noticed tiny wrinkles around them from smiling and from spending time outdoors. Their driver took a sharp turn, and her companion glanced out the window. "You are not uncomfortable spending the afternoon at the fair, then?"

"No. I'm quite looking forward to it."

He went on to describe a few experiences from past carnivals he'd attended, and suddenly all the awkwardness between them fled.

The driver stopped and opened the small door between his box and the interior. "Afraid I can't get any closer, my lord."

The street was, in fact, packed, and after making arrangements with Reed to return to the same spot in three hours, he set them down amongst the bustling throng.

All manner of Londoners seemed to be in attendance, and Goldie was grateful to have worn boots instead of slippers as the crowd moved along the muddy clearing in the general direction of a large striped tent.

When a few of the more aggressive participants shoved them from behind, Lord Standish took Goldie's hand in his. "I don't want to lose you," he said.

His fingers threaded between hers and their palms clasped together. It felt far more intimate than when he'd taken her arm. Someone jostled them, and the earl shielded her body with his.

Goldie ought not to be so aware of her reaction to this man. But it was impossible not to be.

His protection made her feel special.

It made her feel as though she mattered. Normally such attention was reserved strictly for her older sister. But Nia wasn't here. Lord Standish was courting *her*!

"The vendors are up ahead." He spoke close to her ear.

Goldie nodded, inhaling scents of fried foods and sweets mingled with the unmistakable aroma of too many humans and farm animals. The combination ought to have been off-putting, but amongst the occasional cheers that went up from various booths, along with music being played in the distance, it blended together to create an exhilarating mood.

There was a sense that here, amongst so many games and merchants, anything was possible.

And Goldie was here with a man.

A suitor? Yes, a suitor. Because he'd asked for her hand in marriage. And also…

Because he'd kissed her. *Reed Rutherford had kissed her!*

"Are you hungry? We can stop for a pastry." Reed's low, gravelly voice sent a wave of heat through her.

Sometimes, Goldie thought, she was always hungry. It seemed to be her natural reaction to trying not to eat.

"Are *you* hungry?" she asked. It would be mortifying to eat alone in front of him.

"Indeed. Carnival treats are a must. We'll start with a tart," he edged them to one of the smaller tents that created a sort of alley. One of the first in the long line featured a painted sash hanging above: Miss Mildred's Boulangère.

Spotting their approach, Miss Mildred, a robust woman in a worn, flour-dusted apron, called out. "Raspberry or apple?"

Lord Standish looked to Goldie, brows raised, for an answer.

"Apple," Goldie blurted out, even though both sounded amazing.

"One Apple and one raspberry," he ordered, handing over some coins. "That way, we can both get a taste of each."

The merchant handed two warm, paper-wrapped pockets over. Goldie took hers, and while she debated removing her gloves, Lord Standish bit uninhibitedly into his.

"Uh oh," he said. "This one's yours. But you need to try that one first."

Aware that he was watching her, Goldie lifted it to her mouth and took a nibble. He frowned, however. "Take a real taste."

And then, staring into his eyes, she took a larger bite. Hot raspberry sauce exploded on her tongue. It was delicious.

Or was that only because of the company?

Furthermore, how in the world did this feel nearly as intimate as their kiss yesterday?

When she was finished, he raised a hand to his mouth. "You have a little sauce right..." He pointed to his upper lip. "Here."

Since she was wearing her gloves, her only means of removing it was to use her tongue.

A light in his eyes flared, and when her knees turned to jelly, Goldie dropped her gaze. It was too much.

"Which is your favorite?" he asked after she'd tasted the other tart. Was that a catch in his voice, or was it her imagination?

"I can't decide. They're both delicious." Her own voice came out little more than a whisper.

He cleared his throat. "If we're going to see everything, we'll need to keep moving." And with both her hands occupied now, one with her reticule and the other with the tart, this time, he placed a hand on her back to steer her.

Each small booth offered something unique and colorful—items not sold on Bond Street. The jewelry, although obviously made of paste, gleamed cheerfully amongst silk scarves, bouquets of silk flowers, and every possible kind of candy. She stopped and admired some hair pins but refrained from purchasing anything that she'd need to explain away later. They didn't stop again until they turned the corner.

"A fortune teller?" A slightly crooked sign hung above this particular tent, and the aroma of incense drifted from inside. "Madam Zeta," Goldie said. She'd heard of such people—fortune tellers amongst the *Romani*—but not imagined actually patronizing one. And she never would have if she'd not come out with Lord Standish—*with Reed*—today.

"None of it is real," Reed said. His opinion didn't surprise her. Watching him last summer, she'd deemed him inordinately practical.

It was, she realized, part of what had appealed to her.

"I know," she said with a sigh.

"But you wish to have your fortune read?" he asked.

Goldie pinched her mouth together. *Did she?*

They'd paused just long enough to garner the woman's attention.

"You, sir. Wouldn't you like to know what lies ahead for you and your young woman?" Madam Zeta pointed at them. Painted eyes stared from the fortune teller's ageless face, which was framed by black and silver hair adorned with more than one colorful scarf. Her voice was low and raspy and oddly compelling.

"Only if my young woman wishes to." Reed deferred to Goldie.

"Yes," Goldie answered without hesitation. When would she have such an opportunity again? Likely never. She'd make the most of this magical day while she was out from beneath her father's thumb.

Reed laughed softly, sounding indulgently amused.

Madam Zeta stepped backward. "Please, come inside then." She gestured to her tent, which, unlike most of the others, was made up of very worn, very old-looking canvas. It was just tall enough for Goldie to stand, and Reed ducked in behind her.

Inside, more scarves decorated the walls. A round table sat in the center with three chairs. "What do we do?" Goldie asked.

"Clear your mind, my child, and sit."

How was a person expected to clear their mind? Goldie glanced over at Reed, who shrugged.

This was going to be…

Fun!

TOO EASY

Sunday morning, after learning of the task he was going to have to accomplish, Reed had not once expected he'd enjoy any of it. He'd walked away from the meeting dreading the scheme—for both himself and the lady he'd have to convince.

But showing Goldie around, by God, was... fun. Being with her didn't feel like a task at all.

It had initially, when he'd made his first visit to the Duke of Crossings' Mayfair mansion. But the more time he spent with Lady Gardenia's younger sister, the more he enjoyed himself.

Goldie.

His enjoyment came from enjoying *all* aspects of her. Her personality, which surprised and delighted him, was as voluptuous as her figure. She exuded a welcoming sparkle tempered only by an inordinate lack of vanity.

And now he sat beside her in, of all things, a charlatan's tent.

"*Woo her,*" Caroline had told him this morning. "*Court her.*" His sister's advice, ironically, came easier than he'd imagined.

Because he liked indulging Lady Marigold Hathaway.

The fortune teller made an elaborate display of closing the curtains to the entrance and then wafting a dish of incense around them before taking her seat on the opposite side of the table.

"Are you going to use Tarot cards?" Goldie asked. Reed loved that she didn't feign boredom or sophistication. And in this case, that her curiosity overcame any shyness on her part.

Madam Zeta shook her head. "I am going to seek your fortune in the glass."

"Scrying," Reed supplied, and the older woman shot him an approving glance.

"Yes," the Romani woman confirmed as she slowly and ceremoniously drew the scarf off the table and revealed the glass ball set in the center.

"Oh," Goldie exhaled, and Reed couldn't help smiling. She shifted nervously, and Reed took her hand.

He'd held her hand earlier. It felt natural.

"Do you see people in it?" Goldie leaned forward. The ball was glass but not quite transparent. It was an ideal prop for creating an aura of magic.

"Visions," Madam Zeta answered. "Now, you must be silent, so I can listen to what the spirits have to say today."

Goldie nodded, looking as though she had another question, but then pressed her mouth together.

Enchanting.

The word drifted through his mind. Madam Zeta made a low humming sound, her eyes intent on the ball. Flames from a few candles reflected off the glass, and it seemed to heighten the woman's focus. If nothing else, the older woman was an excellent actress. She would have had decades of practice, of course.

But then, a cool breeze wafted through the room, flickering the candles and stiffening Madam Zeta's spine.

She pinned her gaze on Reed, and even he couldn't escape

the ghost that seemed to slide down his spine. "You have suffered great loss," she said. "But also great gain."

Goldie turned to glance over at him, her brows lifted high, but then just as quickly turned her attention back to the fortune teller.

"And you," Madam Zeta directed her attention to Goldie. "Will be faced with a test. A test of courage. A test of faith. Your happiness depends on passing it."

"What kind of test?" Goldie asked. "What will it be?"

Madam Zeta's dark eyes shuttered and closed, and then she made a great show of distress before opening them again. "You were not to speak. But that is all the spirits have for today, I believe."

"But what does it mean?" Goldie persisted.

"That is for you to discern. I am but a mere vessel." Her accent sounded heavier than it had before.

Reed rose and tugged Goldie to her feet. She was looking confused and more than a little troubled, and damned if that wasn't the opposite of what he wanted for her today.

He shouldn't have agreed to this.

His goal for the day had been to put Goldie at ease, not add to her fear.

"That will be two shillings, my lord."

My lord?

Even as he dug into a pocket, he frowned.

He was wearing his old and comfortable clothing—nothing that gave away his new status. Why would this woman think he was any different from all the other rabble coming through?

Goldie stood beside him, however, looking every inch the lady. He supposed that the fortune teller's assumption about him came from the obvious status of his companion. Yes, that made sense.

She'd gotten lucky when she'd mentioned his loss—and his gain. It was vague enough that it could have applied to anyone.

"My apologies, Goldie," Reed said after they'd exited the tent. "She upset you."

Goldie laughed, but he didn't miss the tremor in it. And then she shook her head. "It's silly. I know. But what do you think she meant? I mean, if any of it was real."

"She's intentionally vague. You ought not to concern yourself with her ramblings. Let's keep going." And then he pointed toward one of the gaming vendors. "Shall I win you a trinket?" Reed was determined to get the afternoon back on track. He needed this young woman to agree to marry him. In order to do that, she needed to feel safe.

So for the next hour, with a good deal of laughter, Reed proceeded to drop enough money to buy at least ten prizes before he finally won her a delicate ring. It was nothing more than paint and paste, but after failing to win it herself, and then cheering him on, she squealed in delight when he finally managed to hit the target three times.

Rigged, of course, and all the more satisfying to have gotten the better of the charlatans.

It was ridiculous, but it was also inordinately entertaining.

The thought that mucking stalls with this woman would be entertaining flitted through his thoughts. Her comments were inordinately clever, and when she laughed, she made little hiccupping sounds, which made him want to make her laugh some more.

He touched her more than was strictly necessary, placing his hand on her waist and twice using his fingertips to brush her hair away from her face. When she spoke, he leaned in closer, drawn by more than her scent.

Simply... drawn to *her*.

By the time he began steering them back to the road where he'd arranged to meet the hackney driver, their mutual attraction now enshrouded them both like a tangible thing. Goldie's eyes sparkled and her cheeks were flushed. She was deliciously attractive and, not bothering to contemplate his motivation, he swung her around a corner and pinned her against a brick wall.

She'd enjoyed their kiss the day before. As had he.

But he needed her consent to *marry* him. Normally he might have used more finesse, but time was running out.

Despite all these thoughts clamoring for his attention, when he stared into eyes swirling with browns and greens and golds, he was simply... lost.

She tilted her head back in invitation. Her kiss was his for the taking.

She tasted of the ale they'd shared earlier, but also sweet and fresh. For an instant, he went back in time—to a time when his most pressing concern had been how to garner the attention of a pretty girl.

Kissing Goldie made him feel young again. It sent surges of inspiration coursing through his veins.

Surges of pleasure, of newness, of hope, and of...

Lust.

"Reed..." She breathed his name and his groin tightened.

The sweet girl in his arms was too pure to be mixed up in any of this, but he was without choices. All he could do was determine to do right by her.

Her very feminine form yielded, and so he held her tighter. He wanted her so much that he nearly forgot where they were.

And what he was doing.

He was courting her—to save his skin and to protect his sisters and mother.

The reminder hit him like a bucket of cold water, and he tore his mouth from hers.

Goldie's lashes fluttered as she opened her eyes to stare up at him trustingly. The smile that stretched her lips was shy.

"That was fun," she said. God, her mouth glistened and her cheeks were flushed a delicate shade of pink.

Reed swallowed hard. Today *had* been fun. She was delightful. Under any other circumstances, he might—but no.

A vision of Newgate stole his breath—much like a hangman's noose would. The possibility of all he stood to lose nearly paralyzed him.

"What's wrong?" Goldie's expression fell. He couldn't allow his desperation to ruin this. And yet, he needed to regroup. Far too much depended on this woman's decision.

"I need to get you home." Already, he'd kept her away too long. And then, experiencing a razor-like panic, he had to ask. "Have you decided?"

"Decided?" She shook her head. "I didn't—Oh, Reed. It's… too soon. Please. I…"

Reed nodded. Of course she couldn't accept his hasty proposal. It wasn't as though she'd fallen madly in love with him.

Or that he'd fallen madly in love with her.

He swallowed hard. She wanted him.

He could take her somewhere private, lie with her, and take the choice out of her hands.

But that wasn't who he was. So instead, he implored her with his gaze. "I need to know by morning."

He threaded his fingers with hers and drew them both back into the crowd. He'd pushed too hard. But just when he believed she'd drop the subject, she spoke up from beside him.

"What kind of marriage would it be?" The question encouraged him.

"Whatever kind you want." And he meant it. "I'll not press you…"

She dipped her chin but didn't look back at him. Did this mean she was considering it?

"And this is all to repair your reputation?" This time she did look over.

He could tell her it was because he was desperate to have

her for his bride—that he'd fallen madly in love. But she deserved the truth.

"The rumors are bad, Goldie." Reed pressed his lips together. "People think I had something to do with the fire. There are people who think I killed them."

"You didn't, of course," she stated confidently. "What utter nonsense."

"How can you be sure?" The question wasn't one that would serve his own purpose, but he was somewhat astounded by her faith in him.

"Because you loved them."

Her response stunned him into silence. He'd loved them once. Yes, but... "I'm mad as hell at them," he practically snarled.

For the past half a decade, Reed had spent most of his time coping with the consequences of his brother's, cousin's, father's, and uncle's reckless behavior. At one point, his uncle had mentioned involving them in the opium wars. When Rupert suggested traveling to India, Reed had talked him out of it.

All the while, they'd made him out to be the villain. They'd referred to him as the *excitement killer*.

And Reed had managed them without complaint. But now...

Reed had failed to manage them on the night of the fire. He'd failed to protect them from themselves...

No doubt, they were all laughing at him from hell. Any love he'd felt for them was gone.

She squeezed his hand and they were walking more slowly now. "But you loved them," she insisted.

"You are wrong about that." He couldn't lie about this, but even so, the words tasted sour in his mouth. "But I did not wish them dead."

"I know." Her simple acceptance seemed to lift a small

amount of the weight off his shoulders. Would it have mattered if she'd doubted him? He barely knew her.

The thought brought him back to his purpose—his hasty proposal.

Their hackney was in sight, just as Reed had requested. "You will give serious consideration to your answer, then?" Time was running out. He couldn't afford to lose himself in maudlin sentimentality.

She exhaled a loud sigh and then winced. Reed assisted her into the vehicle and climbed in behind her.

"If you can find it in yourself to accept, I'll do everything I can to ensure you're comfortable. You'll have my sisters. You'll be a countess…" God, he was practically begging.

"What about love?" Her smile was a sad one. "I know it's not common, but… Despite today, which was absolutely marvelous, you don't really know me. Not that I expect anyone to fall head over heels for me, but I've looked forward to my season—I'd hoped…" she turned her face away from him.

Love?

He should have known. Love was the last thing he'd contemplated in all of this. And yet… She was sweet. He was attracted to her.

"I don't know," he answered her honestly. "I don't want to mislead you. But I suppose it's possible… eventually." She had hoped… Reed had no doubt that given the chance, more than one gentleman of the *ton* would fall for this delightful bundle of sunshine.

A sour sensation followed the thought.

She rolled her lips together and nodded. "And I don't want to mislead you. My father has promised me a season. I've had a wonderful day, almost as though I was truly being courted. I want more of… this. I want… more."

The hackney was moving along swiftly now, separated

from the carnival crowds. Despite the cool temperatures of early spring, Reed felt a drop of sweat trail down his back.

She was on the verge of telling him 'no.'

Reed didn't want to give her false hope. He didn't want to use her so blatantly. Taking her hand in his, he lifted it to his lips.

"Promise me you'll think it over." He pressed a kiss to the back of her fist. "Please."

A pause, and then she nodded. "But you cannot come to my father's house," she said.

"I know." Reed understood. He did. It was too soon. She was too young—too innocent. "Meet me in the park tomorrow morning and give me your answer then?"

She frowned but dipped her chin. "By the trees?" She was not being flippant in her response. Although young and filled with naïve dreams, she could be a somber little thing when the moment demanded it.

He was grateful for that. "Yes."

And then Reed had no choice but to deliver her back to her father. She asked him to set her down a few houses away, and as he bid her farewell, Reed wondered if she would come tomorrow after all.

He only allowed the driver to move on after watching her enter the large mansion down the way, and after she disappeared, an unexpected emptiness filled him.

WAITING

"I can't think of anything more you can do." Caroline hugged her knees to her chest at the opposite end of the settee from Reed. "The duke hasn't any other daughters, as far as I know." Her smile was forced.

"I could have declared my love for her," he said. "Three little words and I could resolve this."

"But you're not that sort of man. You would regret it for the rest of your life. It's one thing to marry her to meet that horrible newspaper man's requirement, but quite another to play with a young woman's emotions. You've been honest, and I'm proud of you for that."

"I kissed her again," he said.

Caroline's brows rose. "Why?"

"I… just did." Because he'd wanted to. "But I'm not in love."

"Hmmm…"

"I barely know the chit, Carol," he said.

"The heart wants what it wants."

"Good Lord," Reed groused. "I'm going to have to keep a close eye on you when you make your come-out. Men are not about hearts, dear sister, and that's all I'll say on the matter."

"Pshaw!" She waved a hand dismissively through the air. "Besides, I'm too old to come out. Melanie and Josephine, on the other hand, will require both of us to watch over them. Melanie struggles to stand up for herself, and Josephine will be an outrageous flirt. I, as the older and wiser sister, shall be their matron companion—a most diligent one at that."

"At three and twenty, you're hardly a matron." Reed appreciated his sister's levity. And the thought struck him that Goldie and Caroline would get along well. In fact, Goldie would fit in with all his sisters.

He ought to have emphasized the benefit while trying to persuade her. But he wondered if he stood a chance regardless. Goldie was young. She was looking forward to her first Season. Aside from consenting to their adventure today, Goldie, he guessed, wasn't the sort to defy authority.

Reed had spent a good deal of time with the Duke of Crossings at Rupert's engagement house party, and the man, for all intents and purposes, was something of a tyrant.

It was insane to imagine Goldie thwarting her father in any matter, really, let alone something so huge as marrying someone without his approval.

He felt a pang in his chest, a burning in his chest. Ever since the fire, he'd experienced this sensation more and more often.

He pushed himself off the settee. There was no way he could just sit around doing nothing, waiting for the hours to pass while Goldie decided his fate.

Rutherford Place was filled with memories, both good and bad. He'd once respected his uncle. Even Rupert had once possessed notable qualities. But the opium had permeated their idleness. And if that hadn't been tragic enough, they'd dragged Randal and their father in as well.

But those two hadn't been forced to imbibe. They'd shown no willpower against it.

Reed paced across the room, jamming his hands into his pockets and turning toward the door.

"Where are you going?" Caroline asked.

"I don't know, but I need out of this house." He could work, of course. But what good would that be? What good was anything he'd done if Helton's original article ran?

Reed wasn't normally one to drink, or gamble, or carouse. But tonight…

"I'm going to the Emporium."

"Reed," Caroline's voice caught him before he was out the door.

"Yes?"

"Be back here by morning. It's not over yet."

TWENTY MINUTES LATER, Reed entered the discreetly placed club for the second time in two days. This time, however, he was not intimidated by these men. He'd enjoy some of the spoils of his title, a title that might very well end up meaningless.

A woman approached, and although Reed acknowledged her with a nod, he refused her company.

And as he approached the bar, a hand landed on his shoulder and a familiar voice said, "You're here."

"Do you *live* here?" Reed countered.

West shrugged. "I've always been a man of excellent tastes." He signaled to a waiter. "Whisky neat?"

It had always been Reed's drink of choice—once he'd graduated from ale and gin, that was. He nodded.

A table opened up and the two of them took a couple of empty chairs at a game of *vingt-et-un*. Reed tossed out a coin but West pushed it back and handed him a gold chip. "It's all done on accounts. The dealers know who you are."

Of course.

Reed would have preferred to wager cold, hard coin. Mere numbers took the sting out of a loss until it came time to settle up.

No wonder so many lords were up to their necks in debt.

For one night, he would play by their rules. In his present frame of mind, however, he'd have to be careful to keep his wits about him.

Reed won the first two hands and then lost the next three. By this time, he and his old friend had downed three drams of what was surely a very expensive Scottish whisky.

"Any luck with Crossings' younger daughter?" West brought the subject up uninvited.

Reed grunted. "She'll give me her answer tomorrow."

"Judging by your sour mood, am I to take it that you're feeling pessimistic?"

"You know me, West." Reed gestured for the dealer to give him another card—which put him over. "Pessimistic to a fault." He didn't want to discuss his pending nuptials… or not pending, as the case may be.

Reed had no wish to discuss his own troubles.

"Now, about your new friends," said Reed, perhaps somewhat clumsily changing the subject. "Winterhope, I understand. You've always been mad for horses. But what the devil are you doing associating with the likes of…" Reed lowered his voice. "Helton? Beckwith? And… Malum?"

West grimaced. The two of them had been close at school, but they'd rarely met up since Reed took on managing his family's estates. West had been a lord, and the two positions didn't facilitate the two meeting up socially.

But now, Reed supposed, they were on equal footing.

"It's Malum's doing, really." West slid his gaze around the room. "I can only say that the four of us have a common objective. Our positions and skills complement the others'. You'd be surprised at what kind of results can be achieved with our collaborative efforts."

Reed knew any endeavor West was involved in would be on the up and up. The other three, however...

"Helton controls the message. Malum controls the money and Beckwith controls the muscle."

"What of you and Winterhope?" Reed asked.

West shifted him an enigmatic glance. "We are the eyes and the ears. But I've already told you too much. Just take note. You're going to marry a young woman under the age of one and twenty, without the approval of her father. How do you think that's going to take place?"

Reed was beginning to understand. And truth be told, he wasn't sure he approved.

"If all goes well," his friend went on, staring at him over the rim of his tumbler, "We'll discuss more details later. You're not without skills yourself, and I think you'll want a part in it."

"An investment?" Reed prodded.

But West merely smiled. "Later, my friend. Once you're a happily settled, happily *married* lord. After hiring a new estate manager to run your properties, you'll need a diversion."

"Right." Reed had a difficult time imagining such a scenario. The waiter appeared and handed them both another drink. As far as the cards, Reed was up.

He dropped the subject and doubled down.

The remainder of the evening progressed in a similar fashion, and by the time Reed arrived back at Rutherford Place, he'd won a few hundred pounds and the eastern sky was a dull blue rather than black. Deep in his cups, disheveled and nearly incoherent, Reed, for the first time, found the services of his valet to be helpful.

"Just make sure I'm respectable by half past eight," he tried not to slur his words as he informed the man.

"That's less than three hours away, my lord."

"Yes, well. I have an important meeting." Reed winced. "With a lady."

"Very well, my lord."

And practically before Reed's head hit the pillow, it seemed, he was being shaken awake. "Time for your bath, my lord."

Oh, hell. Whiling away his time at the Emporium hadn't been his most brilliant idea after all.

∼

Goldie didn't sleep much that night, either. Not because she was carousing, of course, but because she couldn't quiet her thoughts.

She liked Reed very much. Yes, she'd considered herself in love with him last summer, but that had been naïve of her. She had watched him, but she'd not *known* him.

And she was under no misconception that if she accepted his proposal, her father would not only disown her, he'd forbid her from seeing her sister or mother. She'd have to find ways to meet with Nia in secret. And although her father didn't seem to care that much about her, he was still her father.

Her family was far, far from perfect. But they were the only family she had.

They were... all she had.

Goldie flipped over to her other side and punched her pillow.

She was going to have a season, yes, but what if she didn't like any of the men she met? What if none of them asked her to dance? What if, as her father had predicted hundreds of times, no one wanted her?

Reed had said he wanted her.

Her. She was the one he wanted to marry, he'd said.

It was a heady thought.

By morning, she'd changed her mind at least a dozen times, but ultimately, she knew what her answer must be.

One of the maids from downstairs delivered tea shortly after dawn, but by the time Goldie sat up in bed and went to drink it, it had gone cold. She winced and set it back down with a sigh.

If only Reed could court her publicly throughout the Season, get her father's permission, and then propose. It would be so simple.

Such a scenario would be a dream come true.

Only her father would never allow it.

And Reed needed her answer now. It was as though he was laboring under some deadline—as though…

She shook her head.

It was as though he was *afraid*.

But he was an earl now! All he needed to do was show the people of the *ton* the sort of man he was, and the rumors would die down on their own. Wouldn't they?

Because he was not at all like the other men in his family.

Her heart cracked at the thought. Poor, dear Reed. He'd lost so much in the past month. And she could help him.

But…

She swung her feet off the bed, frustrated with her own indecisiveness, and went about preparing for their meeting.

"You will be faced with a test. A test of courage. A test of faith. Your happiness depends on passing it."

Madam Zeta's words had taunted her all night.

Was this the test? It had to be. Was she a coward if she didn't marry him? Was she a coward if she did? And faith in what? Her father? Reed?

Herself?

Goldie shoved one last pin into her coiffure. Updos invariably never contained her hair for very long but this one was going to have to suffice.

No doubt when she returned, at least half her curls would be dangling around her head.

But that wouldn't matter. Goldie's hand shook.

Once she'd given him her answer, she'd return home and have a good cry.

She donned her gloves, drew a shawl about her shoulders, and tiptoed out of her room.

Mr. Bulwark was away from the door when she crept through the foyer.

Perfect.

And as she marched solemnly toward the park, her heart sank with each step. There was only one answer, really. Because he was asking too much—for her to take such an irreversible step required far more courage than she possessed.

FINAL ANSWER

Reed paced back and forth on the path where they'd agreed to meet, avoiding looking into the sunshine thanks to the throbbing behind his eyes, compliments of his indulgences just a few hours before. Despite bathing and drinking a horrid concoction sent up by the cook, his head ached, his stomach churned, and his thoughts weren't as clear as he'd like.

"Reed?" Her voice sounded sweet and fresh as it drifted across the lawn. "Am I late?"

She wore a garish yellow dress, but on her, somehow, it chased his gloom away.

Unfortunately, she wasn't smiling.

He glanced down at his fob. "Right on time, Sunshine." Straightening his shoulders, he braced himself for the worst.

"I won't waste your time with excuses and reasons. Oh, Reed, I'm so sorry. I can't do it." She sounded out of breath, as though she'd been running. "I'm so sorry," she said again.

Reed swallowed hard. It was as he expected. He'd hoped, yes. But had he really imagined this lovely young woman would marry him under such havey-cavey circumstances?

"You've no need to apologize, my lady."

"Goldie. Please, Reed. I am still your friend." She placed a hand on his arm, and he dropped his gaze to study the intricate lace of her gloves.

Friend?

"You are right in your decision." Had he known this all along? Was that why he'd drowned his concerns the night before?

But the lump in his throat felt larger than before—the vise squeezing his chest even tighter.

"You look pale. Will you walk with me?" she asked, and when he didn't move, she dropped her hand. "That is, unless you don't want—"

He reclaimed her hand. "No, I do. I'd be happy to..." He ought to be hastily making his way home. He ought to be frantically searching for some other option.

But there were none, and oddly enough, he wanted a few more minutes in her company. Despite her refusal, this sweet young woman he'd only just come to know was a balm to his soul.

"This way." He vaguely remembered seeing a folly set along a different path, one with a bench. They could sit together. He could simply be in her presence—soak up her peace.

Neither of them spoke until they came to the small clearing.

A friend.

Just as he expected, the folly came into view. It was half covered in vines as though it had been forgotten by the groundskeepers. The bench remained, however, and Reed brushed it off for her to sit.

"I was going to try to persuade you," he said. "By luring you with the sparkling companionship of my sisters." Meeting her eyes, he grinned for the first time that morning.

"That would almost do the trick. I remember Miss Ruther—

I mean, Lady Caroline. She was very kind to me last summer. You have other sisters?"

"They were too young to attend such a house party, but I'm sure you would have gotten on well together," he said, a fond smile lightening his expression. "Melanie, who is nine and ten, isn't nearly as managing as Caroline, and she's the quietest out of the three, but she is the most loyal person I've ever known. And Josephine can almost always make you laugh." Reed fell silent as he pondered the youngest of his sisters. "Not presently, of course. She was our father's favorite."

"Your mother is lovely as well." Goldie sat quietly. "How is she?"

"Devastated, as one might expect." Reed exhaled, recalling his mother over the past few years. She'd watched her husband and eldest son slowly deteriorate—not only physically, but mentally—morally. The tragic deaths ought to have come as a relief. "I think she's mourned them for some time now." The backs of his eyes burned, and he blinked the sensation away.

"As have you?"

"Yes." Damnit. Much more of this and he'd be bawling like a baby.

In the privacy of the crumbling folly, the two of them simply sat and listened to the birds fluttering around outside. Evidence suggested a few nests had been built in the ceiling. It reminded him of their talk the day before.

Had that only been yesterday morning?

"I gave it a good deal of thought, but I don't suppose you care much about my reasons." Goldie's voice, echoing off the stones around them, sounded like a melody.

Reed lifted his head. Her reasons shouldn't really matter, and yet…

They did. *She did.*

She mattered.

"I'd like to hear them."

"Well." She stared down at her hands. "My father is not one to give up a grudge easily. He can be a bear of a man." Reed hated the trembling sound in her voice. She shook her head. "But he's my father. We're supposed to honor our fathers, right?"

Reed grimaced at that notion. He'd once honored his father. In the end, it was his father who'd dishonored his family.

"Just because he's your father doesn't mean he deserves to be honored." Reed spoke of his own sire as much as hers.

Goldie was twisting her gloves in her lap again, something he'd noticed before.

"He would disown me. I'm quite certain. I'm… afraid. I love my sister with all my heart. She's the only person who's ever really understood me. My family is all I've ever known." She stiffened and forced a smile. "So, I'll make my come-out this season and hope some kindly man—one my father approves of —asks for my hand."

"You'll have plenty of suitors," Reed said. Hell, it was possible she'd take the *ton* by storm. With that glorious hair, her mesmerizing eyes, and gorgeous figure…

But there was more to her than her looks.

For some reason, he felt sick at the idea of her with another man. He didn't like the idea of some pompous lord wooing her, courting her.

Touching her.

"When the time comes, don't be hasty in deciding," he went on. "Be as picky as you want to be. Trust me. Flowers will be delivered by the dozens."

This sensation was spurred by more than his personal disappointment. It was spurred by jealousy.

He didn't like it one bit.

She wrinkled her brow. "I think you are wrong about that, but thank you. You're being awfully nice over all this. My father isn't at all calm when he doesn't get his way." She blinked and then bit her lip. "I wish things were different."

They could be.

"You thought I'd be angry?" Reed held her gaze. "Why wouldn't I respect your decision?"

She licked her lips. "Because… I—I'm not giving you what you wanted."

His protective instincts surged to life. "It's about what you want, Goldie. Always remember that." And then, because he couldn't help himself, he reached a hand around her neck. "What do you want, Sunshine?"

He studied her eyes—today there seemed to be more golds than greens and browns. At that moment, he would have given her the world if she asked.

"Tell me," he said.

"I want…" She swallowed hard. "I want…"

"What?"

She dropped her lashes and then barely whispered. "One last kiss."

Reed would have chuckled if he didn't imagine that it might hurt her feelings.

"That," he growled, "I can do." Reed pulled her forward, pressing his mouth against hers.

She shifted on the bench to face him, and in an instant, this kiss deepened into something more than the ones they'd shared before. Because it would be their last? Or because no one was around to interrupt them?

Fitting her against him, he rested one hand just below her breast.

And his blood spiked by at least ten degrees. How had she wedged her way into his affections so easily?

He slid his hand higher and cradled the plump mound. She wore no stays this morning so nothing prevented him from feeling the warmth of her skin. He stroked his thumb around the tip, and her nipple hardened into a tight little bud.

SHE WAS SO SOFT. *Full of goodness!* So inviting.

Innocently enchanting! Something promising existed between the two of them and he was going to have to walk away.

Reed hesitated, torn within.

She fit his hand perfectly, little more than a handful. She arched her back, molding herself against him. "Reed." His name on her lips, followed by a moan, lit a fire in him.

"Goldie," he breathed, trailing his mouth over her chin, down her neck, and to her chest. Like a drowning man, he inhaled her essence. Clean, warm, vanilla-scented woman.

Saying goodbye was all wrong. If he'd met her under different circumstances—if he wasn't on the precipice of utter ruin… She could have been his.

He would have courted her properly. He would have given her everything she deserved.

Instead, he would give her this. Or was he fooling himself? Was he taking it for himself?

This kiss.

"You're beautiful, Goldie. Never doubt that." He leaned forward, and laved his tongue over the sensitive flesh before capturing it—sucking her in and smiling when she exhaled a fluttery sigh.

Pleasuring this innocent young lady was wrong, but it was also right. It was as though the two of them had been discussing this dance since the beginning. Neither could walk away until they'd finished it.

Her fingers threaded through his hair as she melted beneath his touch.

"Reed."

He pulled her legs across his lap and slid his hand under her gown. Yesterday she'd worn practical half-boots. When she'd climbed into the hackney, he'd gotten a glimpse of woolen stockings.

Today her slippers were delicate and her stockings made of silk. He stroked his fingertips up and down the length of one calf.

"You don't know how many times I…" She trembled. Was she embarrassed?

"You thought of this?" Reed finished for her.

She nodded into his neck. "Last summer… I grew rather fond of you."

Reed's breath caught. Was she going to change her mind?

But she was right. She would lose everything. It wouldn't be fair to make her give it all up. "What do you want, Goldie?" he asked instead.

"This. I just want this."

He walked his fingers higher on her leg.

"This?"

She nodded again.

"Look at me, sweetheart." This had nothing to do with him marrying her. This was pure, unadulterated attraction.

He would not seduce her into changing her mind. Reed clenched his jaw.

"Yes," she said. Her legs parted in a timeless invitation.

"When you find this husband you're going to land." Reed stroked the silk of her stockings. "Be sure he makes you feel special."

She stared at him silently, her mouth parted as though she had something to say.

But nothing came out.

Reed inched up to where her stockings ended and delicate skin, softer than any silk ever made, beckoned him to keep exploring.

Goldie kept her gaze locked with his. "Yes," she said. And then… "How?"

"Let yourself feel," he said. Reed nudged her thighs wider. Finding delicate curls, he slid his fingers along her folds. He didn't need to ask if she liked this; pleasure flushed her face and her eyes glowed. She licked her lips, her breath hitched, and his fingers were soaked with her arousal.

His cock pushed hard against her bottom but would remain firmly tucked inside his breeches.

Curling his finger, he entered her slowly and watched as her pupils dilated.

Just for her. Just this once. She'd not go into her season like a lamb to the slaughter. She'd know a thing or two of her own needs.

Reed only wished he could use his mouth. And he wished he could know her completely.

But this wasn't love. This was desire—a far more tangible emotion than what she wanted.

The only kind he knew how to match.

"So beautiful," he whispered. "If you were mine, I'd lay you out on my bed, and I'd memorize every inch of you—with my eyes, my hands… and with my mouth."

He added a second finger, relishing in her velvety warmth as her muscles clenched around him. "And then I'd cover you with my weight. I'd lick you, and taste you, and fill you with my cock, making you mine forever."

She closed her eyes and tensed. A teardrop formed at the corner of one eye, and Reed captured it on his tongue. And as she pulsed and squeezed his hand between her thighs, Reed wondered if he'd missed his chance. He could beg her to be his. Promise her the love that mattered so much to her.

What was love, anyway?

He could cajole her, offer her promises. The idea taunted him but he refused to allow it to take hold.

Instead, he kissed the top of her head and after allowing her a moment to catch her breath, he helped straighten her dress.

If he implored her now, it wouldn't be fair.

She pushed herself off him, her legs shaking.

"I should walk you back now," he said.

"Yes. Yes." Her answer was distracted.

Vague.

This time he did not hold her hand, but only watched her footsteps to ensure she made it safely back to the path.

At the street, she seemed to have gathered her wits and turned to look up at him. "Good luck, Reed. I'll never forget you."

"Forget me," he said. "But always remember…"

"What?" She cocked her head.

"That you deserve the best."

Her eyes glistened, but before she could respond, Reed pivoted and practically ran to get away from her.

For her sake.

Because she deserved so much more.

BETRAYED

⌘

Entering her father's home, Goldie walked right past Mr. Bulwark and rushed up to her chamber, where she immediately threw herself facedown onto her bed.

What had she done? What were these feelings?

She was terribly confused as questions echoed in her head. Had she made the mistake Madam Zeta warned her about? Saying goodbye to Reed had certainly felt like a mistake. She thought she'd seen sadness in his eyes, but it could easily have been a reflection of her own emotions. Were these emotions only fleeting?

No!

Because she'd fallen hard last summer, but now she actually *knew* him.

He was kind and understanding. He loved his sisters and mother, and he was everything she'd believed him to be last summer. And more!

But was she prepared to give up the only life she'd ever known? Her sister who was also her best friend?

And then it struck her that even now, she was alone. And their father would find another gentleman to marry Nia.

Nia would leave her soon.

If Goldie did not find a husband, she'd have no choice but to act as companion to her mother and to do her father's bidding.

And despite Reed's insistence that she'd easily land a husband, she'd been led to believe the opposite her entire life.

And if she didn't land a husband, she would never have her own home—or children—or…

She would have no one to kiss her.

Or touch her. She'd live the life of a cold, lonely spinster.

But it was done. She'd given him her answer. What would he do now? No doubt, he'd find some other young lady to pursue—someone whose father would approve.

Imagining Reed holding anyone else with the same tenderness he'd shown her… of him touching another woman intimately, of him kissing anyone but her… was devastating! She swallowed a threatening sob, but a few tears escaped nonetheless.

Closing her eyes, she relived the morning's events over and over in her mind.

His scent and his taste were distinctly unique and utterly unforgettable. He'd not checked his passion when he'd claimed her mouth with his. He'd plundered.

He'd devoured. And Goldie had wanted all of it.

And more.

She ought to feel tawdry by allowing such intimacies, but instead, she felt… Cherished. If he'd proposed again, at that moment, she would have said yes.

Goldie punched a pillow and curled onto her side.

Even in the bustling crowd at the carnival, she'd felt protected.

And now she had disappointed him.

With all these thoughts tumbling around her head, her lack

of sleep from the night before caught up with her and she drifted into a restless sleep.

"Wake up, my lady."

Goldie murmured a protest, but the hand on her shoulder was persistent. "Your father wishes to speak with you."

"Right now?" Goldie rolled over to stare at Nellie, one of the maids from downstairs. "What time is it?"

"Half past eleven."

Being summoned by her father was never a good thing. Had he heard about her outing earlier this morning? Had word of her visit to the carnival somehow gotten back to him?

She rubbed the sleep out of her eyes and pushed herself up to sit.

"Did he say what it was about?" Goldie asked, hating the familiar sick feeling of dread that came with the prospect of one of his talks.

"No, my lady."

The gown she'd donned for her earlier meeting had become too wrinkled for an appearance with her father. Furthermore, a glance in the mirror showed all the ravages of her bout of tears.

Nellie immediately understood Goldie's predicament and rushed across to the wardrobe to remove a new gown. "The water in the bin is fresh. Hold a cool cloth to your eyes," she said.

"Thank you, Nellie." Goldie unfastened the front of her gown and wrestled out of it. "Where is he?"

"He's in the morning room, my lady." Nellie pulled out a muted mint muslin, not one of Goldie's favorites, but she didn't have time to find something else.

Ten minutes later, looking perhaps more tired than usual but otherwise perfectly presentable, Goldie rushed downstairs to join her father at the table where he sat reading the Gazette and drinking tea.

Placed at the right of his plate was a sheet of familiar parchment—a letter—covered with her mother's handwriting.

"You are late." He barely glanced up as Goldie sat in the chair held out for her by a footman.

"Good morning, Father." She quickly glanced at the clock on the mantel to confirm that it was, in fact, still morning. A quarter till noon.

She exhaled. So much had already happened today. But if she were to dwell on her meeting with Reed now, she'd tear up again.

"I received a letter." He frowned.

"Word from Mother?" Goldie asked. "Is she well? Is Nia?"

"Ah, yes," he spoke as though he'd forgotten why he'd called her there. "Both are doing splendidly, as a matter of fact. Lord Dewberry is showing an interest in your sister."

"The duke has a son?" Goldie had met the Duke of Dewberry on a few occasions but didn't remember ever hearing about any offspring. And although Dewberry was only slightly younger than her father, his skin was dry and powdered to hide ever-present scabs, and his eyebrows had grown together into one long line over small, cloudy eyes.

"He's without progeny," her father informed her. "In fact, he's in need of an heir. Your mother believes Nia can expect an offer from him in the near future. Your sister will be a duchess, Marigold."

"But…" Goldie was horrified. "He's so old!" Poor Nia! Marrying Dewberry seemed a worse prospect than marrying Lord Rupert would have been. Nia was young and bright and positively lovely.

Lord Dewberry… was not.

"He is a duke." Her father gave the stare he used to keep his wife and daughters from arguing with him. It was dark and cold, and promised swift retribution if the person on the receiving end posed any further argument. Goldie's stomach clenched.

"Oh." *Poor, poor, Nia!*

"And," her father said, "With Dewberry on the line, she and your mother have decided to remain in Bath indefinitely."

Indefinitely? But they were meant to return to Mayfair any day.

It took Goldie a moment before she comprehended the ramifications of this new information. "You mean until the Season begins?" That would mean delaying Goldie's come-out.

"I said indefinitely, and that is what I meant. In fact, I'm going to send you there to join them. Without your mother and sister here, you have no business in London."

"But my come-out—"

"Was never a good idea." Her father finally looked at her fully. "Come now. You know as well as I that you're not fit for marriage. You're far too opinionated." With the subject dismissed, he glanced down at his fob watch. "There is plenty of daylight for you to begin your journey to Bath today. Be a good girl and pack your belongings at once. I've already ordered Coachman John to ready the carriage. He'll be waiting for you in half an hour."

"But—" Goldie faltered, stunned.

This couldn't be happening!

"I've no companion."

"You'll do well enough. It's not as though you haven't been galivanting around Mayfair on your own these past few weeks." So he had known. And he hadn't really cared.

He simply wanted to be rid of her.

"But I'll have to stay in an inn by myself—"

"Trust me, a gel like you has nothing to worry about. Lock yourself in your chamber when you get there, and don't come out until morning." When she didn't move, he pinned her with that glare again. "You're dismissed, Daughter."

Her father had just rearranged her entire life in less than five minutes. No come-out? No husband? No family?

"You will be faced with a test. A test of courage. A test of faith. Your happiness depends on passing it."

Despite her father's dismissal, Goldie sat frozen.

She'd made the wrong decision! The duke had returned to reading his paper, and as Goldie stared at him, her heart turned cold.

Yes, he was her father. But to him, she wasn't really a daughter. She was a nuisance, an irritating responsibility.

Recollections from this morning's meeting with Reed slammed into her.

She'd made the wrong decision!

And on the heels of that realization, she began plotting a plan to remedy her situation.

If it wasn't already too late.

She went to rise, and a footman drew her chair backward.

"Very well," she said. She moved toward the door, but before she exited, she turned back. "Goodbye, Father."

A lump nearly choked her words, but he didn't notice.

"Hurry along." Her father waved her away.

Which was just as well.

Climbing the stairs back to her room, she blinked away tears.

Her father did not deserve them.

And by the time she had located her valise and begun filling it with belongings she couldn't live without, she was fuming. At her mother, at her father, but also at herself.

She had courage. Scads of it!

Tons of it!

She simply needed to use it. And she would use it to take control of her own life.

She secured the case closed and, with one last glimpse around the room, slipped into the corridor and down the servants' stairs. Once she was sure no one was watching her, she snuck out the garden gate and all but ran to where she remembered Lord Standish's Mayfair townhouse was located —on Hanover Square. Luckily, Nia had pointed it out to her last spring.

It was set back from the street, but grand, and visible from St. George's Cathedral. She would know it when she saw it.

If only she was half as confident that Lord Standish would be there.

Because if he wasn't, she…

Hadn't figured that out yet.

∼

"There must be something we can do. Perhaps I can stir up some other scandal to squash these rumors. Because I refuse to allow my favorite brother to live out the remainder of his life in Newgate." Caroline pinned a stern look on him. "Or worse."

"You'll do nothing of the sort." Reed spoke in stern tones because he wouldn't put it past his sister to do something stupid for him. It wouldn't be the first time. Despite the five years he had on her, she'd stood up for him more than once.

"Perhaps I can talk to Lady Marigold…" Caroline pondered aloud.

Reed contemplated it for half a second. Caroline could be quite persuasive when she put her mind to it. And yet…

Goldie had made her wishes quite clear. By marrying him, she'd have to give up her family. It wouldn't be fair to manipulate her decision.

"No…"

Earlier, after being refused, Reed had walked around the blasted park more times than he could count, first, in an attempt to tamp down his inconvenient arousal, and once he'd succeeded with that, he'd racked his mind in search of another answer to his problem.

He was going to have to speak with West—and Helton, of course. The publisher had seemed somewhat sympathetic, or he would have run the first story already—despite his arm-twisting.

But first, Reed returned to deliver the bad news to Caroline.

Smoothing his hands down his thighs, he pushed himself off the settee and glanced at the clock. Five past one.

He felt ten years older than he had yesterday at this time.

And he couldn't blame it on the alcohol he'd consumed last night. No, he could blame that on the fact that he'd run out of time.

Caroline rose as well. "I'm going to talk with her."

"You'll do no such thing, Caroline. I mean it."

She didn't get the chance to argue because a knock on the drawing room door cut into the conversation. How long would it be before the rumors solidified suspicions? Before the magistrate acted upon them?

"Enter," Reed called out, hearing defeat in his own voice.

The door swung open, and Beasley stepped one foot inside. "There is a lady here, my lord."

Reed stilled. What lady in her right mind would associate with their family right now? "My mother isn't taking visitors," he reminded the man.

"It is not your mother she wishes to see." The butler met Reed's gaze. "Lady Marigold, daughter of the Duke of Crossings, is here to see you."

Reed froze.

"Send her in," he said.

Silence fell when Beasley disappeared until Reed paced across to the window and then turned to meet Caroline's gaze.

"She's changed her mind," Caroline said.

But Reed shook his head, not wishing to get his hopes up.

But they hadn't time to speculate because a moment later, the door opened, and Mr. Beasley escorted Goldie inside—quite a different-looking Goldie than he'd met with this morning.

Gone was her yellow gown and carefully pinned coiffure.

She locked a panicked gaze with his. "Reed—my lord," she said. "I was afraid you wouldn't be here."

Half her curls had come undone, her cheeks were flushed, and her eyes a little puffy—as though she'd either been sleeping or crying.

And she was carrying a valise in one hand.

"My lady," Caroline said.

Goldie's eyes widened as though she hadn't realized anyone else was in the room.

"Oh, Miss Rutherford—my lady," she faltered. "I didn't mean to interrupt." She began walking backward toward the door.

"No!" Caroline was on her feet, taking Goldie's arm and leading her to the settee. "You aren't interrupting anything. Please, sit down. I'll go ask Cook to bring tea."

Reed wasn't used to such a swing of emotions. He felt hopeful that she'd changed her mind, but he was also concerned that something had happened to cause Goldie to appear so harried and… distraught.

Above all, he was relieved to simply see her again.

Paralyzed by the onslaught, he remained by the window until Caroline made her hasty departure.

Goldie shifted so she was facing him. "Have you found someone else?" Lines of worry creased between her lovely eyes and, even holding her valise with one hand, she used the other to pluck nervously at her glove.

"Someone else?" But there was no one else. She'd been the answer to all his problems.

And more.

If anything, Goldie appeared more distraught. "Have you found someone else to marry today? You're an earl, after all. But in case you have not… If… I'd like… I've changed my mind. Reed. I'd like to marry you—that is—if you still want me."

Reed could hardly believe his ears. With a shake of his head, he finally moved across the room and then gingerly lowered himself onto the seat beside her. "You…" He cleared his throat. "You wish to marry me after all? What about your father? What about your come-out?"

She raised her fist to her mouth, and her hazel eyes swam with unshed tears. "They no longer signify."

Something had happened. Reed took her fist in his, lowering it so their hands rested between them. "Of course I still want you." For more reasons than he'd set out with. "I'm…" And then he smiled. "I'm delighted. But only if you are sure."

"I'm sure," she answered emphatically.

Caroline returned at that moment, not bothering to knock. Seeing Goldie's hand in his, however, she hesitated. "Is there to be a wedding after all, then?"

A NEW FAMILY

*R*eed was allowed no time alone with his newly betrothed as Caroline had immediately whisked Goldie upstairs. Which, he supposed, was as it should be.

But although he had matters to attend to himself, not being able to talk to her frustrated him. He wanted to learn more about her reasons for changing her mind. They obviously had something to do with her father. Had the duke discovered that she'd met with him? Had the duke hurt her in some way?

Caroline, however, would take good care of Goldie. Already, Reed heard the sounds of heated water being carried upstairs. Servants scurried about and the house seemed to come alive for the first time since the passing of the old duke.

Thinking there must be much to do, but at a momentary loss as to what any of it might be, Reed returned to his study.

He would send word to West. Yes. And to the church, confirming the prior arrangements. Keeping busy grounded him. Keeping himself occupied was just the ticket.

He retrieved the special license from his top drawer. All he needed to do was fill in Goldie's name.

Marigold.

A glance at the clock on the mantel sent a burst of vigor shooting through his veins. Because, by some miracle, he might just pull this off.

And pulling this off roused an entirely new set of nerves.

Because, it seemed, he was taking a wife.

Tonight.

~

Lady Caroline didn't waste a moment as she all but dragged Goldie upstairs and into a luxurious chamber. "I'd put you in the suite that adjoins Reed's, but my aunt's belongings are yet to have been cleared out. We didn't think it would be necessary so soon." She sent Goldie an apologetic wince and shrug. "But we'll have them removed this afternoon. You'll be needing it after you return from the church this evening."

Church. This evening. Goldie blinked away the dizziness that threatened.

And before she could protest that this suite would be quite sufficient, two other girls appeared.

"Lady Marigold," Caroline said. "May I present my two younger sisters to you—your future sisters-in-law: Lady Melanie and Lady Josephine." Caroline grimaced. "I'm still not quite used to that. We never expected Reed would have the title."

Both were younger versions of their older sister, and equally pretty.

"It is rather exceptional, isn't it?" Goldie clutched her valise in one hand, not sure what to do.

"Are your trunks going to be delivered later?" Lady Josephine asked. Because under normal circumstances, the daughter of a duke would have more than one valise of belongings to bring with her into a marriage.

She'd also have a dowry.

And a church full of guests.

"I… I don't know." Goldie decided to jump right in with the truth. "My father doesn't know I'm here. He wouldn't approve if he did." The thought struck her that if he suspected any of this, he'd likely storm his way inside and challenge her betrothed. He might not consider her feelings as his daughter, but he expected her to follow his rules.

Goldie turned cold at the thought.

"You mustn't worry about that right now," Lady Melanie offered. "By marrying Reed, you'll have his full protection. And you'll soon learn that he doesn't take his responsibilities lightly."

"You will also have free reign with his accounts at all the local shops," Lady Josephine added with a wink.

"Josie…" Lady Caroline shot her younger sister a stern look.

In the hours that followed, Goldie couldn't help but acknowledge that all three girls were every bit as friendly as Reed had said, and his descriptions of their characters, surprisingly accurate.

Lady Caroline managed everything with an abundance of enthusiasm, while Lady Melanie offered quiet support, and the youngest taunted her older sisters that she would be Reed and Goldie's children's favorite aunt.

Whereupon Lady Caroline sent her youngest sister a second stern look before asking the maid to bring tea.

In the quiet that settled after, Lady Melanie spoke. "Your father shouldn't blame Reed, you know. It's not his fault the hunting lodge burnt down."

Goldie hugged her arms in front of her. Everything was happening so fast.

"Let's not talk about that today." Lady Caroline took charge again. "Lady Marigold has a wedding to prepare for." And as though responding to a cue, a footman knocked, and with a nod of permission, he and three other uniformed men began carrying in steaming buckets of water.

Behind them were two maids, one bringing linens and the other a tray with sponges and soaps.

"Reed had piped water installed at our father's estate—at Breaker's Cottage," Lady Melanie sighed. "He's quite forward-thinking when it comes to practical matters. I'm just happy we won't have to live in this mausoleum after all. Uncle Lucas considered the convenience of modern amenities a waste. He said the expense didn't justify when there were servants to tend to such matters."

"Uncle Lucas didn't care—"

A harsh look from Caroline silenced the youngest yet again. But in the matter of a few minutes, Goldie understood that Reed's sisters were all staunch supporters of their brother.

And although Goldie had already deemed him trustworthy in her own mind, she found it reassuring.

Lady Melanie, however, had mentioned residing elsewhere. "Surely you'll remain here at Rutherford Place?" Goldie asked.

She'd imagined his entire family living here with her and Reed after the wedding, and learning differently, she experienced a jab of disappointment. The prospect of having such lively girls about was something she'd never realized she'd wanted.

"It's because of me." An older woman with salt and pepper hair and piercing blue eyes stood in the open doorway. Dressed in all black—gown, gloves, and veil—the woman could be none other than Reed's mother.

Having endured years of etiquette training, Goldie immediately rose and then dipped into a low curtsey. "I am honored to meet you, ma'am," she said.

Technically, as the daughter of a duke, Goldie outranked Mrs. Rutherford. But this woman was going to be her mother-in-law. And having turned her back on her own family by agreeing to marry Reed, Goldie would do whatever she could to find favor with his family.

Her new family.

Because Goldie needed… people.

"The pleasure is mine." Mrs. Rutherford's gaze drifted around to her three daughters. "We are grateful, all of us." The servants moved silently as the girls nodded solemnly. "Your decision cannot have been an easy one."

Goldie wished she could think of an appropriate response but only gulped. In the end, she hadn't had much choice.

Her own father had taken that from her.

"As for returning to my husband's residence," Reed's mother continued, "It's best you begin your marriage as mistress of your own home. We promise to be out of your way first thing in the morning."

Goldie would have protested, but Mrs. Rutherford's demeanor was firm. And from what the girls had said earlier, the newly widowed lady no doubt simply wanted to return to her own home.

Reed's mother reiterated her welcome and then disappeared as quickly as she'd arrived. And over the next several hours, Goldie was sure she would have been overwhelmed if she didn't like Reed's sisters so much.

Lady Caroline had sent for a modiste, who brought several gowns for Goldie to try, and then just as quickly swooshed away to alter the one that all three sisters deemed perfect.

After languishing in a hot bath, Goldie barely touched her tea and sandwiches as she sat by the fire while Caroline styled her hair. And upon donning the lovely emerald gown that now fit her perfectly, Goldie even agreed to a very small amount of rouge on her cheeks and lips.

Sometime in the midst of it all, Reed had sent up a missive informing them that the wedding had been scheduled for seven in the evening. They'd all sit down to a special dinner afterward. And although a part of Goldie may have wished otherwise, time flew.

"I'm going to leave you alone now so I can get ready." Caroline was the last sister to remain in Goldie's chamber. "But if you have need of anything else, I'm three doors to the left."

"All of you are coming?" Goldie asked, imagining herself and Reed in the magnificent cathedral all alone.

"We wouldn't miss it for the world." Caroline smiled as she backed out the door. "Just remember, the third chamber on the left. I'm there if you need anything."

When the door closed behind the older girl, Goldie exhaled a loud sigh. Just this morning, she'd been determined to make the most of her season, and now…

She stared at herself in the looking glass.

Now, she hardly recognized herself. The gown, made up of luxurious silk, fit in a way that emphasized her bosom and hips, nipping in at the waist so that it appeared smaller than usual. And Caroline had done her hair so that the curls seemed deliberate rather than chaotic.

Even her eyes looked brighter. Was that because of Reed?

Or because she was terrified?

An army of nerves exploded in her chest.

Not only had she run away, but she was going to marry a man whom her father disapproved of vehemently.

Her sister would not be there to see it, nor would her mother.

Goldie paced across the room and stared out the window down at the gardener's hut, which was set just on the edge of what would be lush gardens come April.

She would be the mistress of this house. Lady Standish.

A countess!

What would her life look like by then?

Her stomach lurched, sending her rushing over to the chamber pot where she wretched up most of the food she'd consumed earlier. Thank heavens the girls, her future sisters, were not there to witness it.

After wiping her mouth and cleaning her teeth, she lowered herself onto a chair and bent forward. When a knock sounded, assuming it would be Caroline again, she glanced up. "Come in."

But it was not Caroline. It was Reed. She drank in the sight of him, hoping to find the thousands of reassurances she needed.

He'd changed into a formal jacket, and his thick dark hair was combed away from his face. The cravat he wore tilted a little to one side, but that only added to his looks. In fact, each time she saw him, he appeared more handsome than before.

"Is it time already?" She sat up.

Reed shook his head. "Not quite, but I wanted a few minutes alone with you." He kept his glistening blue gaze fixed on her as he drew up a chair.

"I like your mother," Goldie burst out.

Reed smiled softly. "She likes you too."

"And your sisters," she added. Why did she feel so awkward all of a sudden? Why, just that morning, he'd had his hand up her gown, doing unspeakable things!

"They adore you." He held her gaze, looking open, inviting any questions. "You look beautiful, but how *are* you?" She'd heard about people gazing into one another's souls but never believed it could happen until that moment.

She had nothing to hide from this man, which was odd, and yet, fitting.

"This is… all happening so fast," Goldie admitted.

"I'd go about it differently, but—"

"I know. It's important to squash the rumors."

"Yes." He dipped his chin. "But it will also stir up a new scandal."

"Which is precisely the point," Goldie supplied. She understood all of this. His mother had thanked her. His sisters had welcomed her with open arms.

By marrying him, she was helping him. But she hoped there would be more to their marriage. She was betting her life on it.

"By stirring up a scandal, it's possible your father will issue a challenge. If he does, how would you like me to handle him? I'm not unwilling to face him, but he is your father. What would *you* have me do?" All his focus was on her, making every inch of her skin come to life.

Goldie flicked her gaze to his mouth, and then down to his hands. Remembering the way he'd touched her earlier. Her breasts tightened with an achy sensation.

But he was asking her how she'd have him deal with her father.

"I'd rather neither of you killed the other," she said.

Even if her father had shown he possessed no regard for her feelings.

"If he calls me out, the choice of weapons will be mine. Details can be arranged so that neither of us ends up pushing up daisies."

Goldie tried to imagine her father in a duel—on her behalf.

And she couldn't see it. "He won't call you out, so you shouldn't worry about it. Now, if you were marrying Nia instead of me, then he would demand satisfaction." She sent him a rueful smile. "But you did not ask Nia to marry you. You asked me."

"I asked you." His gaze warmed her. "I didn't think I'd see you again," he admitted. "Did something happen?"

Embarrassment warmed her cheeks. She'd been so certain her reasoning had been sound. "My father decided to send me to join Nia and my mother." And then she added, "Today."

"No debut?"

She shook her head. "I won't change my mind again. I'm not fickle."

"You have every right to change your mind as many times as you'd like. This is your future, after all. And in this instance, I'll admit to being glad of it."

His gentle tones and kind understanding flustered her. "T-thank you," she managed.

"Are you nervous?" he asked.

She would not mention that she'd lost the contents of her stomach just ten minutes before he arrived. Besides, now that he was here, sitting in front of her…

"A little," she admitted. Suddenly she wanted to be in his arms again. She wanted him to kiss her again.

He glanced at the fob watch hanging from his coat and then rose and offered his hand. "Come here," he said.

This.

This was why she would marry him. Deep down, she sensed a special understanding between the two of them. She had little reason to trust it, but it was enough.

She took his hand and allowed him to pull her up to stand.

Rather than take her into his arms as she'd wanted, however, he spun her around so her back faced his front.

He placed both his hands on her shoulders and began rubbing the chords of her muscles.

"Oh," she sighed as the tension she hadn't even realized was there began easing away.

"My sisters can be quite… exuberant. But they mean well," he said. "I hope they didn't wear you out."

"Quite the opposite." Goldie relaxed into him. "I like them." Had she said that already?

He chuckled as his fingertips moved up her neck, smoothing over her skin and sliding into her hair.

"I'm glad."

Goldie waited a moment and then asked, "Are you nervous?"

"I'm relieved." Did his voice catch?

His answer was an odd one, but then, nothing about their arrangement was normal, was it? He'd kissed her. He'd told her he wanted her.

He'd touched her intimately.

But the marriage was to serve a greater purpose. Naïve though she was, she realized that for him to marry just over a month after the deaths in his family would be great fodder for gossip.

And he would protect her as much as possible—from the gossip, but also from her father.

She was putting a tremendous amount of trust in him.

"People are going to say horrid things about me." She hadn't thought all of this through. She'd lived most of her life under a cloak of invisibility. How would it feel to be the center of attention—and not the sort of attention one usually vied for?

"Yes." He did not deny it. "We'll remain in London for a few weeks into the Season. Unless you would prefer otherwise."

"What will people say?" Goldie asked.

"They'll say I couldn't resist your charms. They'll say that your new husband is little more than a common estate manager who couldn't keep his desire in check." His fingers trailed over her shoulders now, slowly, and his voice definitely sounded lower. "The bachelors will berate me for stealing you away before any of them had a chance to vie for your affections themselves."

She felt his breath near her ear.

"Surely not—ah…"

His mouth landed on her neck and her heart fluttered. When he dropped his hands from her hair and wound them around her waist, she melted like butter.

"They will be right in their speculation," he added.

The only nerves bothering her now were those of arousal. Nerves he'd awakened that craved more of his touch…

But just as she went to spin around in his arms, a knock

sounded at her door. "Goldie! We should be going down now." It was Caroline.

Goldie jumped away from Reed just before the door opened.

Caroline, a very astute young woman, glanced between the two of them with a knowing look. "Definitely time to be going. Reed, you walk over ahead of us. Your bride should be the last to arrive. It's already bad enough you've seen her on your wedding day."

Goldie barely stifled a hysterical laugh at this.

Because she hadn't even realized it was her wedding day until after noon.

"You will be faced with a test. A test of courage. A test of faith. Your happiness depends on passing it."

She only hoped this was the right test.

And she hoped Madam Zeta hadn't been spouting a bunch of nonsense.

AT THE ALTAR

*R*eed tugged at his cravat, staring down the long aisle dividing the pews at St. George's Cathedral.

From the altar.

Where he stood waiting for his bride!

"Helton will be outraged, initially." West spoke softly from where he stood beside Reed.

"But he did not specify which of Crossings' daughters I was to marry."

"No, he did not," West answered. "But it was implied."

"A little late to second guess, wouldn't you agree?" Reed lifted his chin and stretched his shoulders. Now was not the time to question his choice of bride. He'd known it was a gamble—she'd been his only option, really.

"You have the ring?"

"For the tenth time, yes." West chuckled, and his amused tone echoed off the walls of this revered house of worship, which was mostly empty.

Reed winced. If this church were a ship, it would be listing to the groom's side, where a smattering of guests sat—mostly his sisters and mother, but a few of his mother's sisters as well.

The pews on the bride's side gleamed shining and empty.

A bride who was the daughter of a duke.

Since she wasn't yet one and twenty, her father's signature would have been forged. Reed had not courted her as she deserved, let alone met with Crossings.

Reed tugged at his cravat, but that didn't loosen the squeezing in his chest.

It was wrong on so many levels, but there was nothing Reed could do about it now. He'd have to make it up to her sometime in the future.

Movement at the back caught his attention, and the door pushed open. Caroline stepped inside first. She'd happily volunteered to act as a witness.

And after his sister had arrived at the altar and stepped aside, Reed shifted his gaze to the back of the church and caught sight of Goldie. She stood in the open door looking alone—exposed. Even from a distance, he saw her hesitation. Was she having second thoughts?

But then she straightened her shoulders and stepped forward.

He'd seen her gown already, when he'd gone to her chamber earlier, but it radiated more brilliantly in the flickering candles lit around the sanctuary.

No—it was Goldie who radiated. His breath caught in his throat.

Spending time with her these past few days had lifted his heart like nothing else. The thought took him by surprise.

She'd brought sunshine back into his life.

And as she neared, her features came into focus. Dark lashes fringed her eyes, which danced with that increasingly familiar myriad of golds and greens and browns. He smiled as he noticed her pert little nose, rousing a pink flush to her adorable heart-shaped face.

And then she smiled at him—with lips that were ripe and rosy and far too kissable.

The effect sent heat shooting through his veins, and Reed exhaled. She was more than pretty. She was sweet and intelligent, and more courageous than any woman he'd ever known.

She was defying her father—the Duke of Crossings —*for him.*

Her trusting gaze held his, and he determined then and there that he would do all in his power to prevent her from ever regretting it. She liked his family. That was a good beginning.

And from their approving looks from where they sat on the left side of the church, it was obvious they liked her just as much.

Goldie ignored the empty pews on the bride's side. Was that why she kept her gaze fixed on the altar, on him? She looked so small and vulnerable. A bride ought to have her father at her side. No doubt, she felt the absence of her family.

Unwilling to watch her walking alone a second longer, Reed stepped down from the altar, covered the short distance between them, and reached out for her hand. And as he escorted her the remainder of the distance, he gave her hand a squeeze. *Everything will be fine—better than fine, actually.*

She glanced up at him and his heart swelled. With gratitude? Or was it something else?

In the flickering candlelight from the sconces on the wall, Goldie's complexion took on an ethereal appearance.

He would eternally be grateful that her sister had left London. Goldie was his perfect bride.

Being with her came naturally. Touching her excited him. She'd wanted him to kiss her again before Caroline had barged in. Would she allow him into her bed tonight?

Together they stood before the priest, and the ceremony began.

He'd sat through dozens of wedding services in the past, not absorbing the solemnity or celebration of the vows. But with Goldie, he listened closely, and recited them from his heart.

And when it came time to slide the ring on her finger, he felt an excitement he hadn't expected. Would their wedding night serve up all the promise her kisses had held?

What he'd assumed to be some sort of punishment wasn't a punishment at all. Reed blinked down at their hands. As long as Helton considered Reed marrying Goldie an equally newsworthy story, Reed's worries would be over.

His marriage would have put the suspicions about the fire to rest once and for all.

His bride slid a gold band onto his finger.

Goldie, however, would be tied to him, and be tainted by the scandal as his wife.

Reed was standing in a house of God, his heart racing like any besotted bridegroom, emerging from his family's tragedy at his bride's expense.

He'd garner standing and respect as the new Earl of Standish, by using Goldie.

Everything he'd gained came because the most important men in his life had died.

A wave of utter self-revulsion hit him like a brick wall, and suddenly, all the warmth spun out of the room. And with this onslaught of frost came the dawning realization that…

This was all wrong.

~

GOLDIE HAD THOUGHT she'd be a bundle of nerves walking down the aisle toward her groom. None of her family was in attendance, not even Nia. Her father would have been told she'd disappeared by now. Did he imagine she was simply pouting somewhere? Hiding in the attic like she'd done as a child?

How long before he even bothered looking for her?

But as she walked toward her groom, as Reed's expression came into view, all those thoughts fell away.

Because Reed, her *future husband*, was watching her with hopeful eyes.

With more than hope, was that affection? He was not marrying her for love. He'd made no pretense of that. But he'd kissed her—twice now. He'd touched her intimately.

And he'd confessed to wanting her.

He'd said he didn't want to marry any other woman. His reasons involved dispersing those nasty rumors, so, of course, this marriage was… complicated.

But no one had ever looked at her like that before—like she mattered more than anyone else.

And as the ceremony got underway, she could almost believe that theirs was a love match.

He even seemed to hold her hand longer than necessary after sliding the simple gold band onto her finger.

But then…

After she'd slid a gleaming band on his ring finger, his entire demeanor changed—not in an obvious way, but she was not mistaken. Whereas he'd initially kept his gaze locked with hers, he'd stood through the last part of the service with it averted. He had only looked at her when necessary, and he rushed the kiss on her cheek.

And instead of taking her hand when it was over, pressing his palm against hers as she'd expected, he offered her his arm, his posture stiff.

Removed.

Last-minute cold feet? Did he regret being tied to someone like her?

Goldie forced her smile as she signed the certificate and then accepted congratulations from their few guests.

But Reed seemed only to endure the platitudes. Perhaps he'd gotten a headache. Was it possible he'd eaten something bad?

Despite Rutherford Place being only a handful of steps away, he'd ordered the driver to take them around the park first. But now that they were alone, he'd become even more removed. "Are you all right?" she asked him.

If he was ill, that would explain his strange behavior, would it not?

He'd sat across from her—not beside her.

"Of course." His answer was short. He turned his gaze out the window.

Something was definitely wrong. But what? Had she done something wrong?

Goldie searched her mind, going over everything that had happened that day. He'd held her in his arms just before leaving her chamber earlier. If his sister had not arrived, surely, he'd have kissed her again. Perhaps he'd have done more.

"Have I offended you?" she asked, wishing he'd return to himself—the man she'd come to know.

Although she didn't know him at all, really, and now she was married to him! Goldie fussed at her gloves, the blood in her veins turning ice cold.

"Of course not," he said. "You've been… wonderful. In fact, I don't deserve you." He shot her a look that was perhaps meant to be reassuring, but his smile was not warm. It was… pained.

"It isn't a matter of deserving one another, is it?" Goldie offered tentatively.

"Is it?" The two words came out harsh-sounding, and his jaw clenched. Over the past few days, she'd not once felt uncomfortable talking with him. But something had happened in the middle of their wedding ceremony.

He'd erected some sort of barrier. But why?

Before she could come up with an answer to his derisive question, the driver came to a halt outside of her new home.

Reed pushed the door open. "My sisters have planned a meal—a celebration of sorts. We might as well get this over with."

He climbed out first and then provided her assistance by taking her hand.

Goldie shivered, though, because the gesture felt perfunctory. What on earth had happened? A vise began squeezing her heart, and the last thing she wanted to do was eat.

The only times she lost her appetite were when she was very, very upset.

Dinner should have been enjoyable. His sisters were perfectly lovely and even his mother, who'd temporarily come out of mourning for her surviving son's nuptials, made pleasant conversation.

But Reed had turned sullen—so much so that his sisters and mother made discreet excuses immediately following dessert. After giving Goldie a series of warm hugs and well wishes, all of the ladies disappeared for the night.

Leaving her alone with her new husband.

Reed remained seated at the end of the long table, his gaze fixed on one of the candles. But he wasn't really present. He was gone, hiding behind that wall he'd built between them.

"I'll go upstairs, then." Goldie moved to rise but hesitated. "Unless…" She wanted to ask him to join her but lost the nerve.

"Unless…?" He lifted his eyes to meet hers.

"I mean. Are you… I thought…"

Reed scrubbed a hand down his face, breaking his icy demeanor for the first time in several hours.

Goldie, however, was feeling quite raw and required all her dignity to hold back threatening tears.

She hadn't expected a dramatic declaration of love; however, neither had she expected…

This.

"I've rushed you into all of this," he said.

"I understand—"

"You need time to adjust…" He didn't meet her eyes, however, and dropped his stare back to his plate where his dessert sat untouched. "I won't expect you to fulfill your… wifely duties tonight or anytime soon."

"Oh." Her heart sank.

He *had* rushed her, but…

When she didn't move, he glanced up again. "Is there something else?"

His tone sent a chill down her spine. What had she done? She was a fool, a ridiculous and naïve fool to have married a man on such short acquaintance.

She rose from her chair and straightened her spine. "No. Good night, my lord." And without waiting for an answer, Goldie spun around and swept out the door with as much dignity as she could muster.

She even managed to keep her tears from falling all the way to her chamber. But once inside, for the second time that day, she threw herself onto the bed and cried.

This day, her wedding day, was turning into the worst day of her life.

∽

REED HEARD the words coming out of his mouth. Rude, thoughtless, horrible words that he had no power over.

Because of a tragedy, because of his uncle, his father, and his brother and cousin's abysmal choices, Reed was left with everything. His feet and hands felt numb as a chill washed through him.

It was wrong! It was as though he had gone to sleep in his old life but woken up in an alternate world. Everything was wrong. He should not be the last man standing. He should not be Standish, and damnit, his actions proved he didn't deserve to find happiness with someone so innocent and sweet as Goldie.

He did not deserve the sunshine. He only deserved darkness.

Newgate. It was the perfect punishment for a man like him —a man who benefited from the tragedy of his own blood relations.

The ceremony ought to have been Rupert's. The ceremony ought to have happened on a Saturday morning—not late at night with none of the bride's family present.

But his cousin had perished. Images of Rupert and Randal flashed through his mind: the three of them playing pirates in the woods, and later, noticing pretty girls together. Followed by memories of his father, holding his mother's hand, laughing while they all sat at dinner.

Events that had all taken place before...

There must have been more Reed could have done. He'd known they were flirting with death—with hell. He'd known they were dancing with the devil. Reed ought to have been able to do something to protect them from themselves.

But Reed had failed them. He'd given up.

Watching Goldie, sweet, innocent Goldie, staring up at him with her heart in her eyes had revealed how undeserving he was. Because... Hell and damnation. He liked her!

He more than liked her.

And he'd been anxiously anticipating their wedding night.

But he couldn't go through with it. Not after coercing her into marrying him as he'd done.

Reed flicked his gaze around his uncle's dining room and exhaled.

Goldie had been prepared to go through it for him. She was… perfect. Everything he ever could have imagined. Reed fumbled with his cravat, untying the knot before tossing it onto the table. That chill left him in a cold sweat.

None of it made sense. Because he wanted nothing more than to go to her but… could not.

He burst to his feet. He needed—air. Even though her suite didn't adjoin his, she would be too near. It would be too easy for him to go to her, to pretend he actually deserved any of this.

And so he exited onto the street and walked.

He walked around Mayfair for what felt like hours. He didn't want to go to one of the gentlemen's clubs that would be open. He'd had his share of drinking and gambling the night before.

But the more he walked, the more he knew what he needed to do.

Once decided, he changed his direction and made his way toward Fleet Street.

Lucky for him, the windows in the building that housed the Gazette's offices glowed from inside.

The doors were locked, but with a few solid knocks, one of the clerks peered outside to see who would come at such a late hour. The man wore a long smock over his shirtsleeves and trousers, and most of his thin white hair stood on end while black ink smudged the side of his face.

"You got a story?" The older man scowled at him.

"Something like that," Reed answered. "I need to speak with the earl. With Lord Helton."

"The earl?"

"Maxwell Black."

"Ah, and you are?"

"Standish."

After eyeing Reed for a moment longer, the clerk opened

the door and directed Reed to wait in the foyer. "I'll see if he's here," he added.

Which meant the earl was, in fact, there. Reed paced back and forth across the room. And when a figure appeared at the door, he ought not to have been surprised to see not the earl, but West, standing there.

"I thought you'd be home with your wife," West said. "But seeing as you've apparently made a mess of it already, come on back."

"What makes you think I've made a mess of it?" Reed growled.

"You're here, aren't you?"

Well, Reed could hardly argue with that logic.

Reed followed West as he proceeded to lead him deeper into the building through a sea of cluttered desks and giant machinery. Once through the large work area, they arrived at a heavy door, which West pushed open to reveal Maxwell Black.

The Earl of Helton, reclining with his feet on his desk, wore his spectacles perched on his nose and had a cigar hanging out of his mouth.

And yet the blighter still managed to look every inch the nobleman.

"Standish," Helton spoke around the dangling cheroot. "I understand you're a married man now. What the devil are you doing here?" He dropped his feet and leaned forward.

"I need to annul it." Reed rubbed the back of his neck.

Helton stared at him from over his glasses. "Why would you want to do that?"

"I can't put her through this. Goldie—Lady Marigold—stands to lose her family." Goldie had her own sister, a sister she obviously loved. She didn't need his. How had he done this to such an innocent?

The earl, however, frowned. "Even if I agreed with your reasoning, it's too late. The paper's been put to bed. Printers are shut down, and half the delivery boys have already collected their bundles."

"Catch them," Reed said. "Surely—"

"It's too late, Reed." This came from West. "It's done."

"Besides, it's a good story." Helton reclined again, clasping his hands behind his neck. "And by marrying you, she's out from under Crossings' control. The old bastard doesn't give two figs for his second daughter. The way I see it, you've done her a favor."

But Reed had not done Goldie a favor! He'd used her. He ran a hand through his hair, frustrated. He'd waited too long to see the error of his ways.

"As for your little change of plans, you ought to have come to me first. Don't double-cross me again." Helton scowled but then handed across a folded paper. "Still, the story was front page material."

Reed couldn't look at his duplicity in black and white, but he stuffed it into his pocket anyway. The die was cast. He was no better than the other men in his family.

And yet he lived. He'd rule the Standish estate, provide for the women in his family, and somehow find a way to make it up to Goldie.

"We're heading over to the club. Care to join us?" West asked. Helton rose as well, donning his jacket.

"Hell no," Reed answered. That would only make everything worse.

REVELATIONS

Goldie's eyes flew open and she pushed herself up. She'd been lying awake all night, half-expecting Reed to return, to come knocking on her door, and half-wondering what would happen if she tried returning to her father's house.

She held her breath, and there was the sound again. But it was coming from outside. Sliding off the bed, she tiptoed across her room to the window.

She didn't know what to expect, but the sight below certainly wasn't anything she'd have guessed.

Moonlight reflected off the blade of an axe, which her husband swung in a controlled but violent rhythm.

He'd removed his shirt, and his chest glistened from his exertions.

Freshly cut wood had been stacked neatly against the hut. Wood that had not been there earlier that day.

But that was not what caught her attention.

It was his expression. Earlier, he'd appeared cold and dismissive. Now, he appeared to be a man... tortured.

And a possibility niggled at her.

He'd treated her like a stranger, almost, and she'd assumed it was because he was heartless.

But after a night of contemplating all the facts, she dismissed that explanation.

Reed? Heartless? Never.

"You've been... wonderful. In fact, I don't deserve you." She played the words over and over in her mind. His voice had caught. And he'd not been able to meet her eyes for more than a few seconds.

Less than one month ago, he'd lost half his family in one night. As the new earl, he'd been expected to carry on as if nothing had happened.

"I don't deserve you."

Goldie donned her dressing gown, stepped into her slippers, and hoped she remembered the way to the servants' exit so she could get to him. Left. Yes, and then right. And then through the kitchens.

Four men had died.

Four men who, although undisciplined and immoral human beings, had been constants in Reed's life. And then Reed had become Standish.

She stepped outside but then paused. What if she was wrong?

What if his cold demeanor was not because he'd felt undeserving?

But what if she was right?

She forced herself to cross the lawn and then follow the sounds of the axe splitting wood, around the path to the gardener's hut.

At first, uncertain and doubting herself, she simply stood back, observing. His motions were steady but fierce. Most pieces of wood split all the way through on the first swing.

He didn't notice her for a while, but when she crossed her arms to keep from shivering, he stilled.

"Go back inside, Goldie." He didn't look at her, but stood motionless.

"You said you were all right. You lied to me," she said.

Finally, he turned to face her. "I didn't."

Goldie inhaled a sharp breath. She'd never seen a man like this before and it took all of Goldie's focus to concentrate on this conversation rather than his sinewy chest and abdomen. He was…

Spectacular.

"You were happy at the church." She was taking a chance with her guess. "Right up until you realized you were not."

He shook his head, but at least he wasn't telling her to go away again.

"I saw it in your eyes," she insisted.

Reed shook his head and then swung the axe, causing his muscles to ripple and flex as he split a giant log in half. "It's not right." Was there a hint of uncertainty in his voice?

"What isn't right?"

"Any of it." He dropped the axe and bent forward, resting his hands on his knees, staring at the ground. A shudder ran through his form, and his breaths sounded loud in the early morning silence. "I knew they were tempting fate. I could have joined them that night. If I'd been there, I could have put it out. If I was there, it might not even have happened."

"The fire," she said and then exhaled. Of course.

Her father had believed the rumors. He'd been convinced Reed had set it—that Reed had taken advantage of the other men's addictions in a manner that he would benefit. Not once had she believed the rumors could be true.

"A senseless fire. And now, they are not just gone, they are… dead. They haven't traveled to the continent—nor are they languishing in some opium den. They're…" He frowned. "They're *dead*." The words were little more than a whisper.

Goldie approached him cautiously and, steeling herself,

reached out to touch his arm. "You couldn't save them. Not if they didn't want saving. Oh, Reed…"

"I should miss them. I should be devastated. But instead, I'm… I'm Standish now!" He rose, and the pain in his eyes was almost too much for Goldie to bear. "I'm the fucking Earl of Standish."

In that instant, Goldie knew she'd been right. In the weeks following the fire, he'd not allowed himself to grieve properly. But worse than that, Reed didn't believe he deserved to be the earl.

He had been happy in the church, but then decided that he didn't deserve *her*.

He didn't believe he *deserved* to be happy.

"Yes. You are Standish now," she said. "And you'll bring honor to your family's title."

His arm trembled beneath her hand.

In an unexpected burst, he tore himself away from her and, lifting the axe in the air, threw it with such force that the blade sunk at least an inch into the exterior of the gardener's hut.

"Reed," Goldie grabbed hold of his arm again. "I'm so sorry."

He did not resist her, so she stepped closer and slid her hand up his other arm.

"I'm so sorry. I'm so sorry," she chanted as he began to shake.

This time he did not push her away.

He slid his hands down and around her waist and buried his face in her neck. "You don't deserve to be chained to a man like me. I'm… I was raised to manage estates, not rule them. You're the daughter of a duke, and I used you—"

"You didn't use me," Goldie cut him off, comforting him with all her might, and yet, still, she couldn't stop his shaking.

"I wasn't fair to you.'

"I came here on my own. It was my decision. Because… Oh, Reed! I *like* the man who manages estates."

"You shouldn't." He pulled her closer.

"But I do!"

And as though her words broke some wicked spell, he claimed her mouth, losing himself in her kiss like a man who'd just discovered a reason to live.

And the shaking stopped.

TOGETHER

This woman possessed magic. Her words brought relief, but it was her embrace that removed the weight from his chest. She'd reignited that sliver of hope he'd thought extinguished forever.

"My sunshine." Reed plundered her sweet mouth with his, half out of his mind with wanting her. How had she gotten under his skin like this?

"I'm sorry," he breathed and a tremor ran through him.

Her arms tightened around him.

"It doesn't matter if you're an earl or a merchant or a king," she murmured against his mouth. "I wanted to marry you." Her words struck the heart of his desires from all directions.

"And I wanted you." He stared down at her in wonder. She was his bride!

It was time he made her his wife.

He lifted her into his arms and delighted in her surprised squeal.

"We're going inside?" she asked.

"We're going inside."

She wound one arm around his neck, clinging to his

shoulder with the other one, and then buried her face against him.

"I don't want to be alone," she said.

Already marching toward the servants' entrance, Reed's breath hitched. "You want our marriage to be a real one." He was fairly certain he knew the answer, but just to be sure…

"Yes." She emphasized her answer with a short nod. "I do."

It was all he needed to hear, and highly motivated, he pushed his chamber door open within moments.

Torn between his need to have her—now!—and his desire to make love to her slowly, to memorize each curve and slant of her body, he hesitated for a fraction of a second.

Goldie wiggled, and he lowered her feet to the floor.

She dragged her hand down his chest, and he realized that he was already half-naked. Not ten minutes before, he'd had sweat pouring off him.

This was their wedding night. He ought to have presented himself in a silk dressing robe, fresh from a bath. "I should clean up first. You deserve better than—"

"I don't want better. I want you like this." Moonlight slanted across her face enough to show the uptilt of her lips.

Her palm pressed flat against his sternum, and she had not stepped away.

"I should wash." But he didn't move. And his voice sounded more animal than human. When had his sweet sunshine become a seductress?

"Light a flint," she said.

Her wish, at that moment, was his command.

Moving quickly, albeit a little clumsily, Reed adjusted his breeches, which had become considerably tighter, and then struck the flint and lit candles on the dresser and the desk by the window.

Goldie was at the wash basin, dampening a linen. Turning to face him, she gestured toward a chair. "Sit for me."

Mesmerized by her voice, Reed did as she asked.

And then, with slow, tantalizing strokes, his virgin bride began to bathe his torso.

"You are a good man, Reed." She dragged the cloth from shoulder to shoulder, taking her time. "You care about your sisters. And your mother." She scrubbed the back of his neck. "And you did everything you could for your uncle."

Reed tilted his head forward, hypnotized by her touch.

"And for your cousin." She dragged the linen down one arm.

"For your father and brother," she added, moving around to his front. "You did everything you could."

Her hands crept around to his chest. And then, sliding the cloth lower, she teased the line of his breeches, her mouth inches from his ear. "And that is good enough. You are good enough. You are everything I've ever wanted."

His patience evaporated.

She'd married him because she had *wanted* to. Reed shot out of the chair, spun around, and captured her mouth with his. He tasted her, devoured her mouth even as he walked her backward toward the bed.

She wanted this as badly as he did. The time for words was over.

She was his *wife.*

His beloved wife!

And with shaking hands, he untied her dressing gown, sliding it off her shoulders, kissing every inch of skin, determined to memorize her—her mouth, her chin, her jaw.

She tasted like sunshine. So beautiful. Perfect. Sexy as hell. He wasn't sure if he spoke the words that flashed through his mind as he lifted her onto the bed. He couldn't savor her and talk at the same time.

And with every touch, she moaned and blossomed, arching toward him, helping him remove her gown, surrendering all.

Reed explored the tender flesh of her belly, licking his way up to her breasts. And once there, he felt like a starving man at a banquet.

More to taste—more to fill his hands.

Her hands had deftly unfastened his falls and he shifted so she could draw them down.

But she was untouched.

"We should go slow." He barely managed. *It was her first time!*

"Don't you dare." Even as she spoke, she shoved his breeches off his ankles in a deft maneuver with her feet.

"You need to be ready," he said, chuckling, but also serious. He would never hurt this woman. She'd come along when he'd needed her most. He would give her…

Everything.

"I *am* ready. I'm more than ready." Her hands explored his back, and then timidly moved to his buttocks. "I've been ready forever."

Reed reached between her legs, smiling when his fingers slid easily along her folds. She was soaked.

For him.

Reed pushed one finger inside, gently stroking the walls of her channel, and her breath hitched.

"Do you know you are perfect?"

"I'm not," she answered.

"Perfect." He added a second finger. "Everything about you."

Even as her muscles tightened around him, she shook her head.

"*I'm not.*"

He had some work to do with this one—with his sweet ray of sunshine.

There were so many things he wanted to do with her. Reed pushed himself onto his elbows, holding his weight up until she opened her eyes, looking confused.

"You're perfect for me," he said. "Admit it."

"You're perfect for me." She smiled. Lush lips, plump and glistening from his kisses.

Reed nudged his hips forward, teasing her seam with the crown of his cock. "Perfect." His gaze flicked from her mouth to her eyes.

"For me," she said.

"Perfect," he said again, pushing himself forward just enough to stretch her opening, and then pulling back again.

"Perfect," she breathed, lifting her hips, demanding more.

He pushed farther inside. "For me," he said.

"For me," she echoed, taking him deeper.

Reed thrust harder, and her inner flesh tightened around him. The tempo increased, and their slow dance took on a primal rhythm.

Never had he lost himself so completely in a woman, but with Goldie, he submerged himself. He ached to feel her everywhere, to claim her completely, and he had no doubt she wanted the same.

~

GOLDIE THOUGHT she'd be shy with her groom when the time finally came to allow him to exercise his husbandly rights.

But that was not the case at all.

His kisses only made her want more. She hadn't been nervous when he'd disrobed her. In fact, she'd helped him. And she'd had no reservations in disrobing him.

Because having seen his upper half unclothed, she'd wanted *more.*

More of *him.*

Him inside of her. *More of him everywhere.*

When he'd pushed through, she'd felt a twinge, but had otherwise been overwhelmed by everything else. Would she have felt like this with any other man?

No.

Because she *loved* him. She'd fallen halfway in love with him last summer. She'd handed him the rest of her heart over these past few days.

He had not turned cold today because he regretted marrying her, but because of the exact opposite—because he had *not* regretted marrying her!

He buried his face in her neck and she ran her fingers through his hair.

He was beautiful… so very beautiful.

And he wanted *her*.

And knowing that made all the difference in the world.

She widened her legs, willing him deeper. She wanted to feel him everywhere, stretching, rubbing.

He was her husband, and he was making love to her.

And then she lost the ability to think about anything at all—anything other than the aching pleasure that tantalized and then crashed over her.

"There you go, sweetheart. Just like that. Just like that." Reed murmured, thrusting harder, deeper, growling. He held himself inside, the deepest yet, and his liquid heat warmed her from inside.

His seed.

He was her husband now, in every sense of the word.

THE ARTICLE

Goldie felt the sunlight slanting inside the room, but didn't open her eyes.

Neither she nor Reed had gotten much sleep the night before. After the first time, Reed had snuggled behind her, pulling her back against his front, and Goldie had expected to sleep.

But then she'd felt his staff nudging her, nestled between her thighs. Reed's hands had come back to life as well.

And his mouth.

"Relax," he had whispered against her neck.

He'd made love to her a second time, hooking her thigh over his arm and entering her from behind, penetrating her with deep, loving strokes.

The second time had begun with a lazy rhythm but turned just as frantic as the first.

And the third… He'd wrapped her in his arms and then rolled her over so that she was in control, essentially riding him.

No, Goldie smiled to herself; neither of them would be getting out of this bed anytime soon.

But when she reached her hand out to find him, however, he wasn't there.

Her husband's bed was a rather large bed, larger than any she'd ever seen, so she rolled toward the direction she expected him to be…

And opened her eyes.

Because this giant bed, aside from her, was empty.

She frowned and sat up. Would a gentleman go riding on the morning after his wedding night?

The thought reminded her of the last time he'd brought her to climax—when she'd done the riding, eventually collapsing on top of him, exhaling and still incoherent from the dizzying heights he'd taken her to.

And she may or may not have said something about *loving* him. She winced.

Reed had… kissed the top of her head. At the time, she'd thought nothing of it. But had she spoken too soon? Last night had been spectacular. It had been a revelation as to all that marriage could be.

For her.

Had it been the same for him?

Goldie glanced around the room. If it *had* been the same for him, then why had he left?

She trailed her gaze around to where her night rail lay, torn. No wonder it had come off so easily. His jacket and shirt from the garden were casually draped over a matching chair.

Had Reed gone out to collect them?

On the floor lay a folded newspaper.

A copy of the Gazette.

She slipped off the bed, and not at all comfortable moving about his chamber while naked in the harsh light of day, slipped into her dressing gown and then fetched the paper from the floor.

But before she could tuck it back into his jacket, the headline caught her eye.

"Standish secretly marries Crossings' daughter."

Good heavens! There must have been a reporter at the wedding. She'd expected this, but not so soon.

She glanced toward the mantel. It was just after noon.

Had her father summoned Reed already? It was possible, although not likely, that he'd challenged her new husband to a duel.

Frowning, she lifted the paper closer to read it. The first paragraph mentioned his uncle and the tragedy suffered by the Rutherford family followed by a brief description of Lord Rupert's engagement to Nia.

Goldie continued reading.

"And disregarding any pretense of mourning, the new Earl of Standish has taken Lady Gardenia for his own wife. But was this a love match? Lady Gardenia was one of the most highly sought-after debutantes to enter the marriage mart last Season, and as the daughter of the Duke of Crossings, could have married any man of her choosing. The new earl cannot be as bad as the rumors suggest, can he, if he obtained the former Diamond's consent?

Goldie frowned.

Taken *Lady Gardenia* for his wife? But… Nia wasn't even in London!

She thought back to the first day Reed had come to her father's house—asking for Nia!

Reed had told her that he needed to marry, and then he'd asked her to be his wife. And he'd done nothing to mislead her as to the urgency required…

But.

Goldie swallowed hard. He had first come to her father's house looking for *Nia*. When she'd refused to give him her sister's location, he'd gone away looking defeated.

It had not been until the next day that he'd shown any interest in Goldie.

She read through the article again, hating the way it made her feel.

"*I want you,*" Reed had said. She'd stupidly believed that she had been his first choice.

Her hand began shaking as the truth washed over her. She had been her husband's *second* choice.

With Nia away, she had been his *only* choice. Of course he'd not wanted any other debutante! That would hardly make as good a story as marrying the Duke of Crossings' daughter—or one of them, anyhow.

She shook her head, confused. He hadn't exactly lied to her, but he'd kissed her. And… more.

She'd told him she loved him!

A wave of humiliation crashed over her. But of course! He'd wanted Nia first. She'd been a fool to imagine otherwise—blinded by her own infatuation.

The door creaked, and Goldie dragged her gaze across the room to see Reed peering inside, looking disheveled and windblown, but no less devastatingly handsome than he had the night before.

"You're awake." His devilish smile would have swept her doubts away if they weren't so very, very heavy. Something in her expression made him pause and look her over more thoroughly. "Is something wrong?" He stepped inside and closed the door behind him. "I'm a monster. Three times! What the devil was I thinking? Are you sore, Sunshine?"

In answer, Goldie held up the paper.

"It says you married Nia." She felt dead inside. She'd been so certain she'd done the right thing.

Reed stilled. "But I married you."

"You wanted Nia first, didn't you?" Goldie almost kept her voice from breaking. She didn't want to cry right now. She wanted answers. "Just, please, tell me the truth." She could hardly look at him. His lie by omission hurt terribly.

The knowledge that she was nothing more than a consolation, a second choice, brought with it a far too familiar pain. It had been bad enough to come second with her parents, being her husband's second choice was even worse. The thought stabbed her.

Reed exhaled and then ran a hand through his hair. "They wanted the story to be about your sister, yes."

Silence filled the room, and then Goldie heard him moving two chairs together. "Let me explain, please. Here, sit down."

Goldie grudgingly allowed him to steer her to the chair and then lowered herself onto it. "One of the maids is bringing tea," he said. "And I brought you these." A small, brown paper-wrapped bundle appeared in her line of sight.

She didn't look up, watching instead as his elegant hands unfolded the paper. Before she saw them, the aroma filled her nostrils.

Which confused her further. "Pastries?"

"I went to the carnival this morning. The Boulangère hadn't opened yet, but I persuaded Miss Mildred to sell me a few fresh out of her ovens."

He had gone all the way to the carnival this morning to purchase a few pastries?

For her?

"That wasn't necessary." She didn't want to place more meaning on the gesture than he intended.

Reed sat the pastries on a nearby table and then took the other chair, the one he'd placed directly in front of her. "I can explain."

Words that didn't hold all that much promise in her experience.

He gently worked the newspaper out of her lifeless fingers and skimmed the contents of the article. When he got to the part about her sister, he uttered a curse, low, but not so low that she couldn't make it out.

Only then did he speak again. "Idiots got the name wrong," he muttered. And then, "Goldie, look at me, please?"

She couldn't help herself—he was impossible to resist.

"I wish you would have told me," she said. "At least then—"

"I didn't want to get married at all," he cut her off. "The publisher at the Gazette was going to run an article that would fuel the rumors surrounding the deaths—serious speculation that I'd killed the men in my family, my predecessors. But a few days ago, he sent for me. Said he would cut that article if I provided the paper with another scandal instead."

"By marrying your cousin's betrothed."

"By marrying *Crossings' daughter*, but yes, his intentions were for me to marry your sister. And initially, it was what I set out to do." He reached across the few inches that separated their knees to take her hands. "Goldie. I never wanted to marry your sister. I didn't want to marry at all."

Goldie squeezed her eyes shut. So far he wasn't making her feel any better.

"But there you were. Everything I never knew I wanted."

Everything I never knew I wanted?

She opened her eyes.

He moved one of his hands to her chin, tipping it back so she had no choice but to hold his gaze. "I was wrong not to explain everything to you first. But everything had to happen quickly and I didn't quite understand it myself. God, when I saw you walking down the aisle toward me…" His pupils grew large, nearly edging the blue out of his eyes completely. "I realized I was the luckiest man alive."

When she kept silent, he added, "That's what sent me into a tailspin—that in addition to inheriting a title I don't see as rightfully mine, I had somehow found you—the woman of my heart. I love you, Goldie. I know you'll think I'm crazy—it's only been a few days. And I've questioned my sanity more than once this morning. But I love you. I…"

He cradled her cheek in his palm. "You have somehow managed to become my everything. You were never second choice, my love. Out of every woman in the entire kingdom, I only want you."

Goldie exhaled a partial sob. "Not just because I'm Crossings' daughter."

"You're much more than that. It doesn't matter if you're the daughter of a duke or a merchant or the king. I want *you*, sweetheart. Only you."

Goldie searched his eyes, so clear, so genuine. This time, the sob that escaped was one of relief. Reed didn't allow a single tear to fall before scooping her onto his lap. This close, Goldie absorbed the tremble that pulsed through him.

"You love me," she said.

"With all my heart." His warm breath fanned across her cheek.

She lowered her lashes and plucked at the button on his jacket. "In case you didn't realize it yet, I love you too." She rubbed her hand over his chest.

He inhaled sharply. "Then you'd better get back into that bed."

Goldie didn't need to ask why, as she was seated firmly on his lap and was growing rather familiar with the workings of his masculine appendage.

"But what about the pastries?" She couldn't help teasing him.

"They'll be put to good use, sweetheart." He lowered her onto the mattress and then shucked off his jacket. "Now, where did we leave off last night?"

AN UNHAPPY PAPA

"I'm not sure I'll ever walk again." Reed's arms collapsed and before his weight could land on his new bride, he rolled and tucked her into his side.

"You will." She let out a little giggle, her fingertip drawing circles on his chest, and then sighed. "Because I like that."

"You do, eh?" He wasn't so tired that he couldn't push himself onto one elbow and gaze at her. "That's excellent news." Would he ever get enough of her? Unfortunately, just as he'd leaned forward to give in to temptation yet again, a distant pounding intruded.

Followed by servants scurrying about, and eventually, a demanding voice. Goldie went still beside him.

"Where is my daughter?"

She shot up. "My father!" Her sweet eyes suddenly filled with not only concern, but *fear*. And Reed wasn't about to stand for that. He jumped out of the bed and hastily stepped into his trousers.

"You cannot go up there, your grace!" Mr. Beasley's voice carried little authority in a feeble attempt to stop an angry duke and rapid footsteps on the stairs proved how ineffective the butler's resistance had been.

And Goldie looked even more terrified.

Reed reached out a hand. "I'll deal with him. I'm not going to let anything happen to you."

She'd barely nodded when the door flew open, crashing into the adjacent wall, causing a painting to fall to the floor.

Reed's shirt remained untucked and his breeches unfastened as he faced Goldie's irate father. Duke or not, this was not acceptable!

If Crossings was anyone but his beloved's father, Reed would have pummeled the man for charging into his bedchamber—on the morning after his wedding, no less!

"Get dressed," Crossings addressed Goldie first and then turned to Reed. "I first believed there was no truth to the article. Even after the maids told me you hadn't slept in your bed, I couldn't quite believe it. But I ought to have known, with you sneaking out of the manor, galivanting around all of London like a common whore—"

"Out! Now!" Reed cut the man off before he could go on. "You and I will discuss this downstairs."

But Crossings was one of those men unaccustomed to taking orders from anyone else, let alone a former estate manager. The duke's eyes darted to Reed and he wrinkled his nose as though sensing something foul.

"You and I won't be discussing anything. The magistrates, however, will have something to say about such a man as you, already suspected of murder, kidnapping an innocent girl—ruining her!"

"He didn't kidnap me!" Goldie insisted.

Reed squared his shoulders. "If you are not willing to meet me in my study today, then we can meet in the park at dawn tomorrow."

The duke blinked, as though experiencing a hint of doubt, but then pushed Reed further.

"Lady Marigold is my daughter. Since I can no longer use her to make valuable connections, I'll have her save me from having to pay for a companion for her mother. So hand over what is mine, sir. We know the marriage is a farce." The duke's eyes narrowed, a layer of perspiration on his upper lip from the heat of his anger, and perhaps from running up the stairs. But when he took a step toward the bed, where Goldie sat clutching the sheets to her chest, Reed grasped his arm.

And ignoring the duke's rant, he repeated the man's options. "My study or the park, your grace?"

Judging by the vitriol that so easily rolled off the duke's tongue, Reed suspected this sort of treatment was not uncommon. And damned if Helton hadn't been right in his assessment that Reed had saved Goldie from her own father.

"Please, Father?" Goldie's voice nearly shattered Reed's heart. Because he understood all too well what if was like to love a person who would only disappoint you again and again. "I chose to marry him."

"Today, or dawn tomorrow?" Reed persisted.

"You seriously want to meet me on a field of honor, over Marigold?"

"To the death, if necessary."

The duke paled.

"Your daughter is an amazing woman. She is not only beautiful and intelligent, but she's courageous, compassionate, and everything a man could want in his wife." Reed focused all his attention on Goldie, holding her gaze with his. "I love her."

She dipped her chin and appeared to blink away tears.

Reed turned back to the duke. "If you want her back, you're going to have to fight me for her. Unless, that is, she wants to go with you." Reed met Goldie's gaze again.

He didn't want to give her the option. She was his wife. She wasn't going anywhere! At the same time, he needed to be sure that, upon seeing her father, she wasn't having doubts. Because Reed had coerced her. The duke's signature on the marriage certificate had been forged.

But more than anything, Reed wanted her to be happy.

"I want to stay with you, Reed." There wasn't even a trace of doubt in her voice.

"If you stay with this pathetic excuse for a man," Crossings said, "You will forever be dead to me. You will be dead to your mother. You will be dead to your sister. You will never be welcome in my home again or that of anyone who knows what's good for them."

"I understand." Goldie squared her shoulders, looking quite dignified, actually, as she sat in bed wearing nothing more than the sheets. A riot of golden curls dangled around her face and her cheeks were raw from his beard, and in that moment, Reed could not have felt prouder to have her as his wife. "Please go."

The duke hesitated, but before he could hurt his daughter any more, Reed stepped forward. And for the final time, he gave the duke a choice. "My study, your grace, or the park? Choice of weapons will be yours and our seconds can hash out the details this evening."

The duke appeared flustered, but only for a moment.

"You're not worth the trouble of a duel, Standish. Neither is she. You want her? Fine. Send the contracts to my solicitors and you can have her. As of today, I only have one daughter." He whipped himself around and exited more abruptly than he'd appeared.

And Reed did not stop him.

The meeting would have happened eventually, he just wished Goldie hadn't had to witness it.

Closing the door, Reed turned back to Goldie. "I'm sorry you had to hear that."

But she was shaking her head. "No. I think it's something I

needed. I'll never wonder if I hurt him by leaving. I'll never wonder if I was a poor excuse for a daughter. I loved him. I tried my best to please him, but he didn't see me as a daughter. I was nothing more than a chess piece for him to move around." She held out a hand. "I'm no longer one of his pawns. Thank you."

Reed was across the room in an instant, pressing her small hand to his lips. "You never need thank me for anything." He frowned. "And if you want to see your sister and mother, I'll find a way."

"I'd like that. Not right away. Because I'm sure he'll be watching them." But she tilted her head. "You would have fought him? For me?"

"I would never let him have you. He's a duke who, unfortunately, also happens to be a bully. I figured the best way to get him to back down was to call his bluff."

"You knew he wouldn't accept your challenge?"

"I suspected he wouldn't." Reed turned her hand and placed a kiss on her palm. "I wouldn't have killed him if he had, because you said you didn't want him dead. But he would have lost. And he would have regretted it."

She shivered, and Reed climbed onto the bed and took her in his arms. And that's how he held her until she squirmed and looked up at him.

"Reed?" she said. "Is there anything to eat? I'm starving."

Reed laughed, relieved to hear that optimism in her voice. How she'd kept it so long with Crossings for a father, he couldn't say, but he was more than grateful to have found her.

The two of them still had battles to fight, but they would face them as a team. And together, they'd find not only happiness, but joy.

"Mr. Beasley said there would be a tray in the butler's pantry," he murmured. But he made no move to leave the bed and when she tilted her head back with parted lips, it was an invitation he couldn't ignore.

"Reed?" she said as her hands curled around his neck. "I thought we wouldn't do this anymore today."

Reed made a mental note to thank not only West, but Helton and Malum for their… suggestion that he marry.

And then he lurched, pinning her onto the pillow with a growl. "I never said that."

And another full hour passed before the two of them, her in nothing more than her dressing gown, and Reed wearing only his breeches, located the tray of food and sat down for their first real meal as husband and wife.

It was the perfect beginning.

***

EPILOGUE

The following day brought a cold, gray drizzle. It also brought the Gazette's printed retraction. On page two, under the simple headline stating Corrections in the bottom left corner, they wrote that Lord Standish's bride was not Lady Gardenia, but was in fact her younger sister, Lady Marigold. They were sorry for any misunderstandings caused by their error.

And although Goldie appreciated having that issue publicly cleared up, she frowned as she read a separate article.

"Something the matter, love?" Reed sat sideways on the loveseat behind her, cradling her between his legs.

"Look here." She pointed. "Nia is engaged to the Duke of Dewberry. That cannot be right, can it?"

"I doubt they'd get two articles wrong in as many days."

"But he's absolutely horrid!" Now that Goldie was happy, she wanted the same for her sister as well. And she couldn't possibly be happy with Dewberry, could she?

"But she wouldn't accept him if she didn't want to, would she?" Reed's question made sense and Goldie slowly nodded.

"True. Perhaps I misjudged him. I sincerely *hope* that I've misjudged him. I was only in his company a few times and I wasn't properly introduced, but he failed to make a good impression either time." She blinked as she read the article. The wedding was to take place three weeks into the Season and would be held at St. George's Cathedral. Just down the street. "I want her to be happy."

"I'll see what I can find out." Goldie's husband of not quite forty-eight hours nuzzled her shoulder with his chin and tightened his arms around her. "Meanwhile, I've been thinking. I know that eventually we'll have to make some sort of nod to society, but for now I want to keep you to myself. What would you think of going away, just the two of us?"

"Now?" She twisted around, surprised. "Are you reading my mind?" Her question was partly serious. Because she would not be invited to her own sister's wedding, and it would hurt to hear about the celebration, to have the ceremony take place a few steps down the street, and yet not be a part of it.

"Where would you want to go?" Reed asked. "Italy? France? The beach?"

"Anywhere so long as it's with you." Goldie leaned into him again, amazed at how comfortable the two of them had become already. A fire burned in the hearth, and although outside looked cold and uninviting, she couldn't possibly feel any warmer.

Or safer.

"You aren't always going to be so easy to live with, are you?"

"I certainly hope not," Goldie teased back.

But there was much to learn about one another, and they could accomplish that far easier away from the scrutiny of the *ton*.

"Are you sure, though? What about your sisters and mother? Won't they feel neglected?" The Rutherford women had done as promised and left the newlyweds to themselves, which Goldie now greatly appreciated. She couldn't help but feel guilty, however, to leave them behind if she and Reed went away on holiday.

"Caroline will be more than happy to look after everyone while we're gone. They'll not begrudge us time together. We'll return before the Season ends and you can make your bow to the queen then if you'd like."

Goldie had forgotten all about making a debut. She was already a married woman, after all! And her husband wanted to take her away so they could be alone.

Together.

"Then I say we go to the beach. I've always wanted to see Cornwall. Nia's told me that the sand there is white, and the sea turquoise."

"Cornwall it is, then," Reed announced. "And once we've returned, we'll see about arranging something for you to see your sister."

"When shall we leave?"

He rubbed his chin thoughtfully before answering. "It didn't escape my notice that when you arrived here two days ago, you only brought a small reticule with you. And as far as I know, no trunks have arrived from your father's house."

"I'm not expecting any, if that's what you're asking." Goldie walked her memory through all the items she wished she'd been able to bring with her: most of the wardrobe her mother had ordered for her come-out, her favorite bonnets, half a dozen pairs of shoes, the few jewels she possessed, not to mention her writing desk…

"I thought I'd take you to the modiste tomorrow—see if she has anything readymade that you can bring on our journey. In addition to those, we can order replacements for the items you've lost."

"Madam Chantal has all my measurements," Goldie said.

"I appreciate that kind of efficiency. Because, you'll need more than just the dresses. We'll make a day of it. *My lady.*"

This time Goldie not only turned her head around, but edged out from his arms so she could sit and face him. And as she stared into his eyes, she had the urge to pinch herself. Because being with him felt too good to be true.

"I imagined becoming a countess, I suppose, as often as you imagined you'd become Standish."

"So not at all," he said.

"Exactly," she said. And she had not forgotten the state he'd been in the night of their wedding. "Are you coming to terms with that yet?" He'd feel the loss for the rest of his life, but she hated that he'd doubted himself.

"I'm not sure I ever will." His cleared his throat. "I hired a new estate manager for my father's estate last week and have been corresponding with my uncle's man at Seabridge Manor as well. I've realized that I can't fulfill my responsibilities as Standish and those of estate manager at the same time. Even so, I'd like to be more involved than my uncle was."

"And yet you're willing to take me away to the beach," she said.

"Pure selfishness on my part." Reed leaned forward and pressed a lazy kiss against her mouth. "So." He broke the kiss and pressed his forehead to hers. "Shopping tomorrow and we depart the day after?"

"You really wish to take me shopping?" Even Lord Rupert had refused to take Nia.

"Besotted husband that I am, I'm not yet willing to let you out of my sight."

"Besotted wife that I am, I am not yet willing to leave it." Which, she supposed, was the perfect reason for the two of them to go away together. They'd have the rest of their lives to deal with other responsibilities; this was the time for them to appreciate and get to know one another better.

In every way.

And she didn't doubt for a minute that Reed would make

good on his promise to make arrangements for her to see Nia. She had not lost everything when she'd run away from her father's home. Rather, she'd escaped an empty future.

And found the man of her dreams.

—The End—

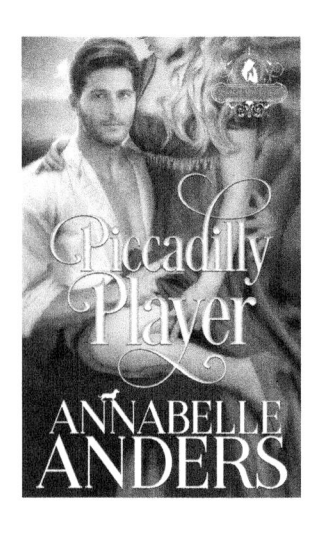

Lady Gardenia has no desire to marry the horrid duke her father has chosen for her, but since her sister's escape, the Duke of Crossings is more domineering than ever.

So when Nia is faced with vowing to love, honor and obey during her wedding ceremony, she is presented with one final choice: marry the horrible Duke of Dewberry, or reach for freedom and run away from her own wedding.

And if she runs, where on earth will she go?

Perhaps the Baron of Westcott can be of assistance…

A sneak peek…

SNEAK PEEK

PICADILLY PLAYER-CHAPTER 1

"I do..."

Standing at the altar with hundreds of pairs of eyes watching her, Lady Gardenia Hathaway barely suppressed a shudder of revulsion while staring across at her groom: the Duke of Dewberry.

The hard glint in his eyes reminded Nia of her father and a hopelessness as gray as the drizzle outside sent a chill ghosting down her spine. Those eyes lacked affection and held only satisfaction. And something else—something more insidious than arrogance.

Control.

Ownership.

"I do." He responded to the bishop through painted lips and then squeezed Nia's hands. His were cold, and the squeeze was unnecessarily tight, nearly causing her to gasp in pain.

But Nia did not look away. This was the man she'd been told to marry, and marry him she would. Because she was the Duke of Crossing's eldest daughter. She'd been known as the diamond of the Season last year.

This was the man of whom she'd pledge herself until death. *This was her duty.*

His cheeks and forehead had been generously caked with thick white powder but the scabs beneath it were still visible.

Ubiquitous scabs that hadn't healed in the two months since she'd first been introduced to him.

The choice of whom she would marry was for her parents to make, and when her mother told her to be nice to the Duke of Dewberry, she'd been all politeness, demure, delicate.

Obedient.

This was who she was, and who she had been for as long as she could remember.

Her parents had decided on her dance master, her piano forte teacher, and other various tutors. And even at the advanced age of twenty, none of her gowns or accessories were purchased unless approved by her mother. But Nia had never complained.

Nia had tried to be the perfect duke's daughter. Now she would be the perfect duke's wife.

The thought reminded her the chat her mother had had with her the night before.

"The first few nights of your marriage will likely be... uncomfortable." Her mother had not met Nia's gaze as she spoke. *"But rest assured, he'll tire of you quickly and return to one his mistresses. As your mother, however, I don't want you to be overly... shocked by the acts he will wish to perform on you. Remember, as his wife, your body becomes his property. And while he does... what he does... know that it won't last long. It won't go on forever. And you will be a duchess!"*

Her mother's speech had kept Nia awake most of the night.

"For how many nights will it be... uncomfortable?" she had asked.

"I cannot say for certain, sometimes just a few days, possibly weeks. To be certain it will end once you conceive. And if the child is a male, you'll never have to endure it again."

But then she'd added, *"Although I suppose he'll want a spare."*

Nia knew about kissing, and had reconciled herself to the practice... But the other things her mother had described sounded disgusting and embarrassing—especially with the man before her!

Nia's stomach, which was already unsettled by her groom's cologne, lurched.

He was her future. *"As his wife, your body becomes his property."* Her mother's words took possession of her entire being and it took all her resilience to maintain her balance.

Because it wasn't right that one person own another. Having her parents dictate her life had been one thing, but to hand herself over to this man... a man she didn't even care for.

A man that revolted her. She felt herself floating up—watching herself dutifully give herself away.

The man standing across from her, at least thirty years her senior, would put his body inside of hers. He would touch her most intimate places.

He could do whatever he wanted. She would be at his mercy.

And he'd want to kiss her with that mouth—that disgusting, foul-smelling and crusted mouth. The thought summoned vomit to the back of her throat for the second time.

How had she allowed matters to come to this?

"And you, Lady Gardenia. Do you take this man..." The priest's voice barely penetrated her suddenly racing thoughts, bringing her back to the present.

"My lady?" The priest addressed her more forcibly. Nia opened her mouth, but nothing came out.

She glanced to where her mother and father sat in the nearest pew of this grand cathedral, a cathedral filled to overflowing with the crème de la crème of the *ton*.

Every one of them watching her, waiting for her to answer.

At the end of this ceremony, she was going to be the

Duchess of Dewberry, not something she'd ever aspired to herself, but it was what her parents expected.

She'd been raised to be the wife of nobility.

With the death of her former fiancé, her mother considered it a boon that she'd been given a second opportunity to land a duke for a husband. Lord Rupert had been heir to a lowly earldom.

This moment was to be the pinnacle of her achievements.

A hint of murmurs rippled through the guests. Nia was supposed to respond to the priest. She realized this. She opened her mouth a second time and still, no sound emerged.

"My lady?" This time, it was Dewberry himself who prompted her, squeezing her hands even more tightly than he had before. She turned back to face her groom.

"I... do..." She slowly began shaking moving her head from side to side. And then she added. "Not."

His hands slackened, in shock likely, and without making a conscious decision to do so, she tore her hands out of his and...

Took flight.

She sprinted back down the aisle. She needed air. She needed to be as far away from Dewberry as possible. And her mother. And her father.

It was instinctual, much as if she was being chased by a viscous animal. Some sixth sense screamed inside that if she were to marry that man, she'd not live to the age of thirty.

She was running for her life.

It didn't matter that she would suffer dearly when they caught up with her.

Because they'd have to catch her first.

She could not imagine returning to her father's home.

The bottoms of her feet flew down the carpeted runner and she dared not look to one side of the other, but only forward— toward the doors she'd entered through earlier.

They represented escape, freedom. Safety.

But she needed to run faster. Already, she sensed someone racing after her. Her father's servants? The duke's nephews? She dared not look back for fear doing so would slow her progress. She didn't even stop at the door, but put her arms out and after a jolt she felt through her entire body, threw them open.

The drizzle had turned to a heavier rain. Lighting flashed, thunder rumbled, and big, cold drops whipped into her face and exposed arms and chest.

Earlier, her mother had mentioned rain was lucky on one's wedding day. For now, it simply made escape all the more difficult.

Because the pavement was slick beneath her slippered feet, and after just a few seconds, the water streaming down her face caught on her lashes, clouding her vision.

But now that she'd escaped the most prestigious St. George's Cathedral, escaped her groom and all those onlookers, where could she go?

Still running, but with no particular destination, she knew she could not go home. Furthermore, every person of whom she might consider a friend had been invited to the wedding and had watched her mad dash from those gleaming pews—wondering perhaps if she would return?

Likely judging her for disgracing her father—dishonoring her groom—two of the most powerful men in all of England.

But…there was one person who had not received an invitation. One person in the world who would understand.

Her younger sister, Marigold.

Goldie had been disowned by her father barely one month ago for marrying the Earl of Standish against his will. And the Earl of Standish lived nearby, on this very street—on Hanover Square…

Nia had visited the house last year—with her former fiancé.

A slamming sounded behind her. The doors of the church closing behind those who would catch up to her.

If her father got ahold of her, he'd show no mercy.

She'd gone years without suffering one of his punishments but she had done the unthinkable. She had embarrassed him. For that he'd not hesitate to bring out his whip.

Even more ominous, he might force her back to that alter, which, knowing her father, was a distinct possibility.

Ignoring the stitch at her side, she pushed herself to run faster.

She sent up a hasty prayer that she was going in the right direction.

Rutherford Place—that was the name of the earl's home. Of her sister's new home.

Goldie, who'd never had to endure their parent's expectations as she had, had witnessed them all the same.

She would understand Nia's plight.

An elegant carriage approached from behind her, and for a moment, thinking it belonged to one of the wedding guests, Nia stumbled, nearly tripping herself.

But it kept driving right on past her before halting several doors down, at the entrance to one of the townhouses. Seemingly unaware of the drama playing out behind him, the elegant gentlemen leapt out and dashed to the door where he lifted his hand. Sounds of the knocker echoed off the streets and the buildings surrounding them.

Nia kept her eyes on both the building and the gentlemen, both familiar.

But of course! He was at Rutherford Place.

Rather than enter, however, upon having a brief word with the butler, he shook his head and dashed back to his carriage and climbed inside.

Nia slowed, and approached the door herself. But before she could sound the knocker, a voice called out from the street. "I'm afraid you'll be disappointed as well," the man called. "They're still on their honeymoon."

Devastation washed over Nia as her heart nearly lodged itself in her throat. Terror followed when she heard footsteps pounding distantly behind her.

"Up ahead! Ho, there! Stop that woman!" One of them shouted.

Nia did not have to look to see that it was her father's men. She did not have to look to know that she was on the verge of losing her newfound freedom.

In what she could only describe as abject desperation, she raced toward the gentleman's carriage.

Before he could close the door behind him, she grasped the handle, and with no time to fuss with the step, threw herself onto the floor of the carriage, scurrying on her knees to close the door behind her while keeping herself low enough not to be visible through the windows.

To say that she'd startled the gentleman passenger would be the height of understatements. But she hadn't time to explain.

"Please, tell your driver to go!" she begged. "My life depends on it."

The man hesitated only a moment, studying her with hazel eyes. Having come to some sort of decision, he raised a hand and pounded on the roof.

"Drive! Now!" He yelled, his gaze still pinned on her.

The coach lurched, and just as the voices outside grew louder, the vehicle began moving. Oh, so very slowly at first, eventually gaining speed.

She didn't allow herself to breathe until the voices outside faded altogether.

At which point, she tucked herself into a ball...

And burst into tears.

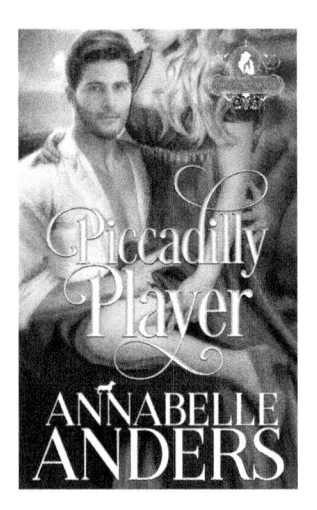

RESERVE YOUR COPY TODAY! - releases May 2, 2023

THE RAKES OF ROTTEN ROW.

Hanover Square Spare
The Earl of Standish

Piccadilly Player
Westcott's story

Fleet Street Scoundrel
Maxwell Black's story

Pall Mall Peer
Winterhope's story

Bond Street Bachelor
Mr. Beckworth's story

Regent Street Rogue
The Duke of Malum's Story

Other Popular Series by Annabelle Anders

Devilish Debutantes

The Regency Cocky Gents

Miss Primm's Secret School for Budding Bluestockings

And more!

Learn about all of Annabelle's books at

https://www.annabelleanders.com

ABOUT THE AUTHOR

Married to the same man for over 25 years, I am a mother to three children and two Miniature Wiener dogs.

After owning a business and experiencing considerable success, my husband and I got caught in the financial crisis and lost everything in 2008; our business, our home, even our car.

At this point, I put my B.A. in Poly Sci to use and took work as a waitress and bartender (Insert irony). Unwilling to give up on a professional life, I simultaneously went back to college and obtained a degree in EnergyManagement.

And then the energy market dropped off.

And then my dog died.

I can only be grateful for this series of unfortunate events, for, with nothing to lose and completely demoralized, I sat down and began to write the romance novels which had until then, existed only my imagination. After publishing over twenty novels now, with one having been nominated for RWA's Distinguished ™RITA Award in 2019, I am happy to tell you that I have finally found my place in life.

Thank you so much for being a part of my journey!

To find out more about my books, and also to download a free novella, get all the info at my website!

www.annabelleanders.com

GET A FREE BOOK

Sign up for the news letter and download a book from Annabelle,

For **FREE!**

Sign up at **www.annabelleanders.com**

Printed in Great Britain
by Amazon